WELCOME TO THE DARK HOUSE

LAURIE FARIA STOLARZ

WELCOME TO THE DARK HOUSE

HYPERION

LOS ANGELES · NEW YORK

Printed in the United States of America

First edition

1 3 5 7 9 10 8 6 4 2

G475-5664-5-14121

Library of Congress Cataloging-in-Publication Data

Stolarz, Laurie Faria
    Welcome to the Dark House/Laurie Faria Stolarz.—First edition.
        pages cm
    Summary: "Seven super fans have won the trip of a lifetime to meet the master of horror, legendary film director Justin Blake. But things quickly go from delightfully dark to dangerously deadly, when Ivy, Parker, Shayla, Natalie, Frankie, and Garth find themselves trapped in an abandoned amusement park. To earn a ticket out, they must face their darkest demons one ride at a time"—Provided by publisher.
    ISBN 978-1-4231-8172-9
    [1. Horror stories.   2. Amusement parks—Fiction.]   I. Title.
    PZ7.S8757We 2014
    [Fic]—dc23   2013023992

Reinforced binding

Visit www.hyperionteens.com

For those who face their nightmares
with eyes wide open.

WELCOME TO THE DARK HOUSE

IVY JENSEN

I WAKE WITH A GASP, COVERED IN MY OWN BLOOD. *It's everywhere. Soaking into the bed covers, splattered against the wall, running through the cracks in the hardwood floor, and dripping over my fingers and hands.*

I touch my stomach, searching for a stab wound. My chest heaves in and out. I'm breathing so hard that it hurts—so hard that I wish for my lungs to collapse and my heart to stop.

I wish that he'd killed me along with them.

The moonlight shines in through the open window, enabling me to see.

I'm in my present-day bedroom.

It's six years later.

I'm seventy miles away from the crime scene.

There is no blood, only sweat. There are no hardwood floors, either. A shag carpet covers unfinished plywood. I reach down and run my fingers over the thick wool threads, just to be sure. Then I check and recheck my comforter, looking at it from different angles. It isn't pink paisley, like the one I had when I was twelve. This one's dark, dark blue.

And there are pale green walls.

And angled ceilings.

And there's an armoire in place of a vanity.

There are no music posters on the wall, nor is there a single reference to the soccer I used to play.

I'm seventy miles away.

It's six years later.

This isn't the same room.

There is no blood.

This was obviously another nightmare.

Still, I make sure of everything by switching on my night table light. I make sure of everything by going through these rituals one more time: by saying the alphabet forward and backward one more time, by touching the pendant around my neck—an aromatherapy necklace that was supposed to be a gift for my mother—one more time.

I'm eighteen years old, not twelve.

I dreamed about him again, because I fear that he'll come back for me one day and do to me what he did to my parents.

Six years ago now.

In a room unlike this one.

Seventy miles away.

SUMMER

Ivy

IT'S SATURDAY AFTERNOON, AND I'M SITTING IN Dr. Donna's office. I've been sitting here, on this same leather chair, surrounded by these same four walls.

On the same day.

At the same hour.

For the same reason.

For the past six years.

I'm not sure if it helps, but I never skip a session, because coming here gives me hope that one day I'll no longer live in fear.

Dr. Donna sits across from me. Her legs are crossed at the

knee, as usual. Her beige leather clog bops up and down to the ticking of her mantel clock as she waits for me to say something. But coming here—doing this—is starting to feel like watching a rerun. It's the same episode on the same channel, with the same actors, saying the same dialogue. Again and again. And again.

DR. DONNA: So, what do you think?

ME: What was the question?

DR. DONNA: It's been six years, Ivy.

ME: Six years and my parents are still dead, and I still feel like I'm rotting away in purgatory, waiting for a killer to determine my fate. Will he come back and kill me today? Or wait until tomorrow? Or will he put it off until next year? Or perhaps he'll surprise me on the ten-year anniversary?

DR. DONNA: And maybe he won't come back at all. You've changed your name. You've changed your address. You've even changed your family.

ME: What choice did I have with that last one?

DR. DONNA: My point is that maybe he's done.

ME: That depends. Do serial killers retire? I think he's waiting for the opportune moment, watching me, studying my habits. Sometimes when I'm shopping in town or walking home from school, I can feel his eyes on me.

DR. DONNA: Do you still think he's the one who sent you the gifts?

ME: I don't *think*; I *know*. He knows what I like. He knows where I live.

DR. DONNA: You're not into makeup, Ivy. So, how do you explain that elaborate cosmetic kit?

ME: And how do *you* explain the paisley-covered journal, the pink soccer jersey, and the Katrina Rowe CD? My love for those things was apparent from my bedroom that night.

DR. DONNA: A lot of people like Katrina Rowe's music, Ivy. And the color pink, paisley designs, and soccer . . . all of those things are popular too . . . as are stars. . . . That star necklace pendant you received, it doesn't get much more generic than that. Anyway, my point is that perhaps a secret admirer sent you the gifts.

ME: Except I haven't played soccer in six years, nor have I listened to Katrina Rowe. And no one who knows me now has any reason to believe that I used to like either.

DR. DONNA: You haven't told a single person? Even in casual conversation?

ME: You still think I'm being paranoid, don't you?

DR. DONNA: I think you have a lot of fear, and I want to help you to defuse it. But I'm not sure what else we can do here. We've talked about that night. We've talked about your nightmares. We've gone over every possible scenario—good and bad—of what could happen in the future.

ME: I need to try something else—to learn to live *with* fear, rather than *in* fear. I mean, lots of people live with fear, right? They put down good money for it. They seek it out from the front row of movie theaters and on roller coasters. They wait in long lines for ghost tours and to go inside haunted houses. They don't let it control their lives.

DR. DONNA: Interesting point. So, how do you propose we get there?

ME: I need to learn from those people. I need to see fear the way they do.

Autumn

IVY

I DON'T KNOW HOW I BECAME A SUBSCRIBER TO THE Nightmare Elf's e-Newsletter. I'm not a fan of the movies, and there's no chance that I'll ever become one, but with a subject line that hints at ridding my nightmares for good, I can't resist rescuing it from my spam box.

TO: IVY JENSEN

FROM: thenightmare.elf@gmail.com

SUBJECT: LAST CHANCE—NIGHTMARES BE GONE CONTEST ALERT

NIGHTMARES BE GONE CONTEST*
ENTER FOR A CHANCE TO MEET LEGENDARY FILM
DIRECTOR JUSTIN BLAKE AND GET A BEHIND-THE-SCENES
LOOK AT HIS CONFIDENTIAL NEW PROJECT

Dear Dark House Dreamers,

> **Greetings from the Nightmare Elf.**
> **I'm sending this note to say,**
> **If you tell me your worst nightmare,**
> **I can make it go away.**
> **Submit your bedtime horror**
> **in a thousand words or less.**
> **Then I'll add it to my sack,**
> **and you'll enter my contest.**

— The Nightmare Elf

Guidelines: Describe your worst nightmare in a thousand
words or less. E-mail it to: thenightmare.elf@gmail.com.

Prize: An all-expenses-paid weekend, including an exclusive,
behind-the-scenes look at the never-before-seen
companion film to the Nightmare Elf movie series,
plus the opportunity to meet Justin Blake.

Deadline: October 31, midnight EDT
Click <u>HERE</u> for Justin Blake's Web site

IN MY HEFTY ELF SACK, YOUR NIGHTMARES WILL KEEP.
BETTER THINK TWICE BEFORE FALLING ASLEEP.

*Must be 18 years or older to enter.

I click on the link for Justin Blake's Web site. I've certainly heard his name before. Most of his titles ring a bell from movie trailers I've seen on TV—those I've tried to avoid with quick reflexes on the clicker.

There's a drop-down menu that lists some of his films and characters:

NOTABLE FILMS	STARRING CHARACTERS
Nightmare Elf	Eureka Dash, Pudgy the Clown, Piper Rizzo, Jason Macomber
Nightmare Elf II: Carson's Return	Farrah Noyes, Danny & Donnie Decker, Meg Beasley, Candy Lane
Nightmare Elf III: Lights Out	Susan Franklin, Max Tarple, the Kramer family (Steven, Lara, Montana, Blakely)
Nightmare Elf IV: Don't Fall Asleep	Eureka Dash, Pudgy the Clown, Janson Dailey, Jed Clive, Betsy Wakefield
Forest of Fright	Sebastian Slayer, the Targo triplets (Ted, Mario, Selena), Joseph Newburger, Frederick Linko
Halls of Horror	Lizzy Greer, the Targo triplets (Ted, Mario, Selena), Glenn Sullivan, Ava Murray

Night Terrors	Little Sally Jacobs, the Baker family (Josie, Carl, Diana), the Robinson family (June, Roger, Daniella)
Night Terrors II	Little Sally Jacobs, Peg & Jessie Miller, the Ernesto family (Thomas, Juanita, Paulina, Kai)
Night Terrors III	Little Sally Jacobs, Jonathan Sumner, Felicia Thomas, Jake Willoby, Reva Foster
Hotel 9	The Scarcella family (Sidney, Darcie, Phillip, Jocelyn), Paige Rossi, Matthew Julian
Hotel 9: Blocked Rooms	Sidney Scarcella, Darcie Scarcella, Midge Sarko, Dorothy Teetlebaum, Carmen Roberge
Hotel 9: Enjoy Your Stay	Sidney Scarcella, Robert Scarcella, Midge Sarko, Emma Corwin, Enrique Batista

I click on the first Nightmare Elf movie title and an elf pops up on the screen: a blond-haired boy dressed in a red suit, a floppy hat, green gloves, and boots that curl up at the toe. With his rosy cheeks and bright blue eyes, he's kind of cute on first glance. But then you notice the way his ears spike up to look like devil horns and the pointy sword that is his tail.

Below him, there's a link with background information on the series' legend. I click on it.

THE LEGEND OF THE DARK HOUSE

One summer, many years ago, the Tucker family went on a camping trip. Deep in the woods, they came across an abandoned cabin with dark clapboard shingles, nestled in a grove of trees. A wooden plaque over the front door read WELCOME TO THE DARK HOUSE, written in red crayon.

The Tuckers decided to stay in the cabin instead of setting up camp. During their stay, six-year-old Tommy began to hear a voice inside his head. He didn't tell his parents—the voice told him not to. Tommy became withdrawn and secretive, often sneaking off into the woods to an old, abandoned storage shed. He called it the nightmare chamber.

"Make sure to visit the chamber three times a day," the voice told him. "There, you will do important work."

The voice belonged to a ten-year-old boy named Carson. While staying at the Dark House three months prior, Carson died from a seizure during a nightmare.

With his beloved elf doll in tow, Tommy would use

a rock to scratch crude images into the walls of the shed—images of people with missing eyes, bleeding mouths, and stakes jammed through their hearts. The Tuckers grew concerned with Tommy's behavior. At the dinner table, he wouldn't speak. He refused to engage in any camping activities, like hiking, swimming, or sitting by the campfire.

One morning, Tommy's father followed him to the abandoned shed and saw the walls. "Explain yourself," he demanded.

"Go to hell," Tommy replied in a deep, slow, creaky voice, per Carson's instructions.

After five days at the Dark House, Mrs. Tucker, so disturbed by her son's worsening behavior, announced that they were cutting their vacation three days short. That same night, she dreamed about a thief in their apartment back home. Tommy had been experiencing nightmares too—recurring visions of a pack of snarling wolves tracking him through the woods.

Carson, still angry that he had died during a nightmare, wanted others to share his fate. His spirit, unable to pass on, had become quite powerful. He could see into

the dreams of anyone who stayed at the Dark House—
and make their nightmares come tragically true.

Tommy was the first victim. He died before the Tuckers finished packing, mauled by a wolf lurking near the nightmare chamber. Weeks later, Mrs. Tucker was killed by an intruder in their home.

After the Tuckers left, only Tommy's elf doll remained. Carson giggled at the sight of it, delighted to have a souvenir. And so he decided to inhabit the doll, dubbing himself the Nightmare Elf. Into his bright red sack Carson would collect the frightful dreams of the Dark House's guests, overjoyed to eventually release their nightmares into reality, making room in his bag for more.

So let this be a warning to all you campers: if you happen across the Dark House in the middle of the night, feel free to stop inside, but do remember this: *IN HIS HEFTY ELF SACK, YOUR NIGHTMARES WILL KEEP. BETTER THINK TWICE BEFORE FALLING ASLEEP.*

IVY

**In a thousand words or less, describe your worst
nightmare.**

Dear Nightmare Elf,

*For the record, I'm not one of your Dark House Dreamers,
nor have I seen even one Nightmare Elf movie—or any of*

Justin Blake's films for that matter—but I've been receiving your e-newsletters for years now, and this last one caught my eye.

I guess you could say that you found me in a weak moment, because the idea of telling an elf my nightmare, and having him magically take it away, sounds pretty amazing right now, especially at four in the morning . . . not that I actually believe a word of your BS. But, at the very least, maybe writing about my nightmare and sending it off into the black hole of cyber-space will trick me into believing that it'll never come back.

So, here goes.

For the past six years I've dreamed that my parents are being murdered in their bedroom across the hall. I'm haunted by this vision because it happened, in real life. I was in my room, sleeping soundly—until I heard it. A thrash-ing sound across the hall.

I sat up, able to hear more noises: a gasp, a sputter, an agonizing moan. Then silence, broken by an unfamiliar male voice: "And now it's your turn. You won't feel a thing."

My mother screamed. "Please, no," she begged. "Don't do this. I have a—"

There isn't a day that goes by that I don't try to guess at her missing words: "I have an idea"? "I have something to tell you"? "I have a daughter"? "I have a wallet full of cash"? I'll never know for sure. Her voice was cut short with a thwack. Then music began to play. String instruments. An eerie blend of violin and viola that reverberated in my heart.

I grabbed the phone on my night table and dialed 9-1-1. "I think someone just killed my parents," I told the operator, hearing a hitch in my throat, hearing words come out of my mouth that no one should ever have to say.

"Where are you?" the operator asked.

"In my room, across the hall."

"Is the person still in the house?"

"I don't know," I replied, keeping my voice low. "I mean, I think so. In my parents' room."

"Okay, I have your address. I'm sending help right over. Can you tell me your name?"

My name? My mind scrambled. My pulse quickened. And suddenly I couldn't get enough air.

"Hello?"

"Ivy," I choked out. "Jensen. My name, that is."

"Okay, Ivy. Listen to me carefully now. Is there a lock on your bedroom door?"

I looked toward the door, no longer able to hear my parents.

"Ivy?" the operator asked. *"Are you on the first floor? Is there a window?"*

I couldn't answer, couldn't think straight. My hands were trembling so furiously, but still I told myself that I wouldn't drop the phone; I'd keep it firmly gripped in my hands.

But then I saw it happen.

In slow motion.

Falling from my fingers.

Bouncing off the bed.

Landing against the hardwood floor.

It made a loud, hard knock. I felt it in my chest. It stopped my breath, stunned my heart, shot an arrow through my brain.

My bedroom light was off, but with the door cracked open, the hallway light leaked into my room and he was able to see me.

"Good evening, Princess," he whispered.

His hair was long and silver, tied back in a low ponytail. His face was covered with stubble. He cocked his head and smiled at me; his lips peeled open, exposing a pointy tongue and crooked teeth.

We both froze, just watching each other, awaiting the other's move—like two wild animals in the night. His eyes were unmistakable: tiny, dark gray, and rimmed with amber-brown. They reminded me of a bird's eyes.

His gaze wandered around my room—my walls, my floor, my bed, my dresser—as if taking everything in. The paisley bed linens, the soccer banners, my fuzzy beanbag chair, all the Katrina Rowe posters hanging above my bed.

A few seconds later, his eyes fixed back on mine, and he smiled wider. "It's very nice to meet you," he said, over-emphasizing every word.

I wanted to throw up. Chills ran down my spine.

Sirens blared in the distance then. He remained in the doorway a few more moments before backing away slowly and fleeing our little yellow house with the white picket fence and the long brick walkway—the place that I'd always called home.

But I knew that wouldn't be the end.

It's now six years later. Those eyes are still out there. And I live in constant fear that the killer will come back for me one day.

In my dreams, he plunges a knife deep into my gut before I can rouse myself. My eyes flutter open, and I'm able to see him. Those birdlike eyes.

His lips peel open and he smiles at me, his pointed

tongue edging out over his jagged, yellow teeth. "You knew I'd come back, didn't you?"

He twists the knife—two full turns—before pulling it out to examine the blade. I touch my stomach, smearing blood on my palms.

That's when I finally wake up.

I haven't told anyone this, but sometimes I wish that he would come back, once and for all. At least then it would be all over.

Ivy

I PUSH THE TIP OF THE BLADE INTO THE SKIN AND make one solid cut. The onion falls in halves. I rip the skin off one of the halves and make a series of cuts, trying to get the layers as thin as possible—a technique only attainable with the sharpest of knives and the precision of an Iron Chef.

I toss the onion shreds into my bowl and look up, nearly awestruck by Enrique's Italian sausage. It's perfectly plump and juicy, slathered in a red chili glaze and stuffed with paprika and oregano.

"Ivy!" my sister Rosie shouts. She jumps in front of the TV screen, distracting me from Enrique's stuffing technique. Rosie is eight years old and in love with SpongeBob. "What are you doing?"

I'm elbow deep in ground pork shoulder and shredded onion. "What does it look like I'm doing?"

She peeks at the TV screen, where Enrique, also dubbed the Spicy Italian Chef (even though he's from Argentina), is dressed in a bib apron and a pair of heart-patterned boxer shorts (his usual TV attire). Though I'm fairly certain his tanned, rippling muscles are part of the ensemble as well. Enrique's explaining the merits of a chunkier sausage over a lengthier one (something about moisture retention), but I'm pretty sure the vast majority of female viewers—not to mention his growing number of male admirers—could care less.

"He's hot," Rosie says. "But shouldn't you be using a fork to mix that stuff?" She points her glue-encrusted fingers into my bowl, coming way too close for my culinary comfort.

"Get out." I swat at her. "Have you been eating glue again?" There are suspicious-looking globules stuck in the corners of her mouth.

"I want a snack," she says, avoiding my question. "And I also want you to read my tea leaves." She takes a jar of dried mint from the spice rack and smacks it down on the counter.

"I'm saving that for Willow's stomach."

"Willow can spend the night doubled over in pain for all I

care. She refuses to let me borrow her blush." Rosie's big brown eyes bulge out in annoyance—a teenager stuck in an eight-year-old's body, Elmer's glue included.

"You're too young for makeup. Go find something productive to do." I flash her my porkified palms in an effort to repulse her, but the porkiness doesn't seem to bother her one bit.

Rosie starts singing extra loud—"*tra la la*"—and flailing her arms, trying to block the TV screen. Meanwhile, Willow, my twelve-year-old sister, comes rushing into the kitchen, saying there's something in the living room that I just *have* to see.

"I'm busy," I tell her.

"Well, get *un*busy," Willow says. "Because Rain and Storm are at it again."

Rain and Storm are my ten-year-old twin brothers, and the reason that people take birth control. I can hear Rain's menacing giggle from the living room. Meanwhile, it seems I've missed at least three of Enrique's steps. He's pouring a cup of red wine vinegar into a separate bowl, but I have absolutely no idea why.

"Come on!" Willow shouts. "They're going to mess up the drapes."

I grab a rag to wipe my hands, moving from behind the island. In doing so, I accidentally bump my bowl. It drops to the floor. Ground pork shoulder falls against the tile with a slimy thud.

"*Ewww,*" Rosie squeals, nibbling glue residue from her fingers. "I'm not eating that."

I hurry into the living room, where Storm and Rain stand with their backs toward me, facing the bay window. "Prepare!" Storm orders.

I hear an all-too-familiar zipping sound.

"Aim!" Storm calls out.

"Fire!" they both shout.

It takes me a second to realize what they're doing. Pee shoots out, hitting the two potted plants in the window, splashing against the soil, and spraying all over the window screens.

"Go to your room!" I yell.

"Well, you *did* tell us to water the plants . . ." Storm argues, still giggling.

"*Now!*" My tone must scare them, because they do as they're told.

"Enrique's all done," Rosie says, from the kitchen. I can already hear the theme song to *SpongeBob.* "*Now* can you get me a snack and read my tea leaves?"

Most other eighteen-year-olds would probably hate my life. But I honestly don't know what I'd do if it weren't for the distraction of this household. I was placed with this family by protective services after my parents were murdered. My foster parents, Apple and Core (self-renamed from Gail and Steve) were a stark contrast to that darkness. Once hippie environmentalists, who named all their children after something in nature, they now need to make a decent living. So, while they go off to work, I stay at home playing full-time nanny for zero-time pay as the eldest of their five kids. School is my only time off, but it's April vacation, and everyone's home.

And *speaking* of April . . . that's my real name, my birth name I should say. But my foster parents changed it to Ivy. We had a renaming ceremony, complete with floral head wreaths, a dip in the lake, and dancing around a fire. I can't say I minded. I wanted to be someone else. I prayed to be someone else. Except for my name, so far my prayers have gone unanswered.

IVY

MY CELL PHONE CHIRPS, ANNOUNCING THAT I HAVE AN e-mail. I pull it from my pocket to check. It's a message from the Nightmare Elf, only this time it didn't go into my spam box. I click on it, remembering the nightmare contest I entered months ago.

TO: IVY JENSEN

FR: thenightmare.elf@gmail.com

SUBJECT: YOU'VE BEEN CHOSEN

2 ATTACHMENTS

Dear Lucky Dark House Dreamer,

In my hefty elf sack, your nightmares now keep.
Better think twice before falling asleep.

—The Nightmare Elf

YOU'VE BEEN CHOSEN

What: To attend an all-expenses-paid weekend, including an exclusive look at director Justin Blake's never-before-seen companion film to the Nightmare Elf movie series, plus the chance to meet Blake himself. Congratulations. Your entry was one of seven selected from over twenty thousand applicants.

Where: Stratten, MN, home of Stratten University. Winners will stay for two nights at a bed & breakfast, chosen specifically by the Nightmare Elf.

When: July 17–19

Transportation: Once your attendance is confirmed with receipt of your registration packet and release form (see attached documents), air and local transportation arrangements will be provided.

RSVP: To reserve your spot, complete the attached forms and return ASAP. Space is limited.

NOW, WHAT ARE YOU WAITING FOR?
PACK YOUR BAGS . . . AND PREPARE FOR
THE SCARE OF YOUR LIFE.

NATALIE SORRENTO

"THIS DISCUSSION IS OVER," MY MOTHER SAYS IN HER 1950s cardigan with an angel pin poked through the fabric.

Did a discussion ever start? There's a smug smile on her face because she thinks she's putting her foot down, but the fact is that her foot—as well as her entire body—has been under my dad's thumb ever since I can remember. My mother doesn't have a single thought that she can actually call her own.

We're sitting at the dining room table. A vase full of tea roses separates us, marking our opposing territories: me against them, thorns against roses.

"You need to think seriously about your future," Dad says. Before retirement, he worked at a plastics factory making BPA-infested food containers. He knocked my mother up when he was in his late fifties—when he was married to someone else, too—and when my mother was twenty-year-old eye candy, working as a teller at the bank. "Do something meaningful with your life," Dad says, as if I could ever compete with Harris.

My brother Harris and I were the product of said affair—twins, born less than sixty seconds apart. Even then we didn't want to leave each other's side.

"This is a once-in-a-lifetime opportunity," I tell them. "My essay stood out over all the other entries."

"Exactly," Dad snaps. "You have potential, but instead you hide it beneath that costume of yours."

"You wouldn't forbid Harris to go," I say; the words come out shaky.

Dad's face blows up like a balloon with too much air. He hates it when I bring up Harris. He hates it when I talk, period.

Before he explodes entirely, I storm to my room, locking the door behind me. The e-mail announcing that I'm one of the winners is still open on my computer. I read it again, making sure that it's real—that it still says what I think it does. My parents can never take that away.

I gaze over at my bookcase, the shelves of which are filled with all of Justin Blake's work, including a copy of *My Nightmare*, his autobiography, in which he talks about feeling like a constant disappointment to his parents. I know that feeling all too well.

I move over to my dresser mirror. There's a desk blotter covering the glass. I take it down, careful where I look; I don't want to see my whole reflection right away. My pulse racing, I pull off my sweatshirt, trying to focus on just the Nightmare Elf tattooed on my belly. When I went to the tattoo parlor, I told the artist to make an extra bulge in the elf's sack for my nightmare—the biggest one of the bunch.

I grab an eyeliner pen off my dresser and, across my belly, beside the elf, I start to write the words *In his hefty elf sack, my nightmare now keeps*, but there isn't enough room. The letters are squished.

I turn sideways to scope out the space on my back. Justin Blake's birth date is tattooed at the very bottom, right in the middle of my underwear line, right below Pudgy the Clown's chain saw.

Harris thinks it was psycho of me to get a man's birthday permanently inked on my skin. But at the time that I got it— just after my mom and sister had girls' night out and "forgot" to invite me—it made perfect sense, because I couldn't thank God enough for placing Justin Blake on this earth.

I angle my back a little more toward the mirror and pull down my underwear to see the couple of tattoos on my ass cheeks: Little Sally Jacobs's skeleton keys and part of the Nightmare Elf's infamous catch phrase, "Better think twice before falling asleep."

Looking at all these tattoos now, I want to tell myself how ballsy I am—how ballsy I was to have gotten them in the first place. But the truth is, they were strategically placed. I could never have gotten them where my parents would see, just like I could never go against their wishes and accept Blake's generous offer.

SUMMER

SHAYLA BELMONT

FINALLY I GET OFF THE PLANE, BUT I'M SO FULL OF negative energy that I can't even stand myself. I'm starving. My muscles ache. The woman sitting next to me in coach wouldn't stop coughing toward the side of my face. Plus, she smelled like bacon, and not the hickory-smoked country kind, more like the kind that's micro-ready in thirty seconds. And, as repulsive as that is, the smell only made me hungrier.

Admittedly, I'd wanted to upgrade to first class, but primo seats are slim to none when you're traveling to East Bum Suck, Minnesota, population: twelve.

I know; I sound disgusting. And I know; I shouldn't complain. I mean, this is a new adventure with new people and new opportunities . . . right? Plus no one twisted my arm to come here. I'm here of my own free will, as part of the Shayla Belmont "make the most of every moment" mission to have a fun and fulfilling life.

This airport is minuscule. People from my flight disperse like ants from repellent. Do they know something I don't? Did I miss the memo on fleeing creepy airports at the proverbial speed of light?

A woman rushes by me, nearly knocking me over.

"Excuse *me*," I call out, suddenly noticing that her pants are way too short, exposing her socks—purple ones with bright pink hearts, just like my best friend Dara's socks. The coincidence gives me a chill.

I gaze toward the windows, but they're blacked out so I can't see. I look around for a security officer or for someone who might be awaiting my arrival, but unfortunately I find neither.

A gnawing sensation eats away at my gut, making me question whether I should turn back around and go home. Still, I grab my bag and head up to the car rental counter. An attendant stands there, but it appears as though things could shut down at any second.

"Can I help you?" the attendant asks. She's at least seventy years old with long white hair and the palest blue eyes I've ever seen. She keeps her focus toward the crown of my head, rather than looking me in the eye.

I run my hand over my hair, wondering if she's admiring my new do. I got my hair straightened at a salon in Chelsea, a place that actually knows how to work with black-girl tresses rather than frying them as crisp as the aforementioned bacon.

"Good afternoon," I say, putting on my best smile. "Someone's supposed to be picking me up, but I'm wondering if there's another level to this airport. Is there a separate waiting area?" I look around some more, but I don't see any stairs, or an escalator.

"Would you like to rent a car?" she asks. "I have midsize sedans or minivans."

"I don't actually need a car." I let out a nervous giggle.

"Are you sure? Because there's a free box of wild rice with every rental." She places a box of rice on the counter and grins at me like it's Christmas, exposing a bright blue tongue and teeth that have browned with age. "This particular grain is native to this area."

I take a deep and mindful breath, as would Shine, my current yoga master, who believes in practicing compassion and kindness rather than succumbing to frustration, judgment, and blame (a practice that proves particularly helpful while riding the New

49

York subway). "Is it always this quiet here?" I ask, attempting to switch gears.

"Quiet?" Her eyes are still fixed on my forehead. Maybe she's blind or has an aversion to making eye contact.

I glance over my shoulder. Aside from the two of us, the airport looks pretty desolate. "Are things more bustling earlier in the day?"

She laughs and snorts at the same time. A spittle of blue drool rolls down her chin. "Have you forgotten where you are? Do you need me to show you a map? US maps also come free with your car rental."

"Wait, *what*?" I ask, utterly confused.

She continues to laugh at me; her eyes roll up farther—I can barely even see them now. There's just a bulging mass of glossy whiteness that reminds me of hard-boiled eggs.

My cell phone rings in my pocket. I fumble for it, but it falls from my grip and clanks to the floor. I pick it up, hoping it didn't break. "Hello?" I answer.

"Hey," Mom says. "You landed."

I move away from the woman, accidentally bumping into a post from behind. There's a phone attached, with a piece of mangled wire dangling out from the bottom, reminding me once again of Dara.

I try to push the wire back inside a hole in the post, but there's too much of it—at least four feet—and it won't all go in.

"Shayla?" Mom asks.

I gaze upward at a support beam. There's a hook sticking out, where one could attach the wire. I picture Dara hanging there, her feet dangling, those heart-patterned socks. Her eyes snap open and stare down at me. Her dark blue finger points in my direction.

"Shayla . . ." Mom calls again.

"Hey," I say, my heart pumping hard. I look away and blink a couple of times. "I'm not so sure about this place."

"Not so sure about Minnesota?" Mom laughs. "You've been to India and Ethiopia, for goodness' sake."

"I know. It's just . . ." I move toward the exit sign at the opposite end of the room. What once appeared like a teensy airport now feels like a major shopping mall. "It's different here."

"Well, of course it's different. You just left the city, *girl*."

I hate it when my mom goes all homegirl on me. "That's not what I mean." I peer back at the support beam. Thankfully, Dara's no longer there.

"Then what?" Mom asks, finally sensing my unease. "Do you want to come home? Just say the word and I'll have something arranged in a matter of minutes."

"Hold on." I move through the exit doors. A shiny black hearse is parked right outside. The driver's-side door opens and a hot-looking guy steps out: midtwenties, airbrushed tan, and dressed in Armani.

"Shayla Belmont?" he asks, holding up my picture—the one I e-mailed with my contest forms. His smile is totally killer.

"Yes," I say. "Are you . . . ?"

"Stefan. And your chariot for the evening, compliments of Justin Blake and Townsend Studios." He opens the door to the backseat. "I hope you'll find things comfortable."

"In a hearse? Are you kidding?"

"I never joke about transporting dead people."

"Except last I checked I was still alive."

"For now, anyway." He winks. "We're waiting for one more person who was on your flight."

I peek inside the hearse, spotting an ice bucket with an array of beverages inside it. There's also a basket of cinema snacks (movie popcorn, Jujyfruits, Sno-Caps, and sourdough pretzels). "Thanks," I say, suddenly remembering my mother on the phone. "I think I'm all set," I tell her as soon as Stefan steps away to load my bags into the back.

"Are you sure? Where are you anyway?"

"I'm just getting picked up from the airport."

"Okay, well call me as soon as you get to the B and B."

"Will do. Love you."

"Love you too, Shay-Shay."

After we hang up, I take a seat inside the car, noticing a movie ticket stub with my name on it. I pick it up to take a closer look. It's actually a welcome note, congratulating me once again on winning, and signed by Justin Blake.

Stefan closes the door behind me and already any reluctance has melted away, replaced with an overwhelming sense of excitement for what's soon to come.

GARTH VADER

"HOLY FREAKING SHIT!" I SHOUT, ABLE TO SEE THE
house in the distance.

The driver looks at me in the rearview mirror. "Is everything
okay, Mr. Vader?"

Okay? I'm practically drooling. "This seriously can't be real."

"I'll take that as a yes."

The house looks just like the one from the movie: the dark
shingled exterior, the shutter-covered windows, the plaque over
the door affirming what I already know.

"Welcome to the Dark House," the driver says.

Goose bumps rip up my arms. It's all I can do not to bust out of the car while it's still in motion. A dilapidated shed—no doubt Tommy Tucker's nightmare chamber—stands in the distance. "Was this place built just for us?" I know for a fact that the movie was originally shot in Hampstead, New Hampshire.

"The house was already here, from what I understand, but it was recently remodeled for your arrival. You'll find that everything about this weekend has been created specifically for this occasion . . . specifically for you winners."

"Wow," I say. "It's definitely the perfect spot." In the middle of nowhere, surrounded by forest. On the annoyingly long ride over from the airport, I think we might've passed three gas stations and two convenience stores, tops.

I grab my bags from the back of the hearse and walk around to the front of the house. The plaque is in direct view now. It's an exact replica of the one from the movie, written in red crayon by Carson, the Nightmare Elf.

"Pretty remarkable, isn't it, Mr. Vader?"

I think the look on my face is agreement enough. I mean, where do I even begin?

All dressed up in his little suit and his little tie, the driver ushers me inside. Here's where things differ from the movie. It's like walking onto the set of *The Real World*, the Dark House edition. The walls are paneled with wood, giving the place the illusion of a cabin, but the furnishings are anything but camplike. There's a huge room with high ceilings. A wide-screen TV hangs on the wall, as does a life-size photo of the mastermind himself. "This is incredible," I say, thinking aloud, noticing how the carpet looks to be at least five inches thick.

There's a plateful of Nightmare Elf cookies on a table in the center of the room. I palm five of them and then look around for a check-in desk, stoked when I don't see one, psyched that this doesn't appear to be a B and B, after all. "Are we alone?" I ask.

"Two others have also arrived—Taylor and Natalie, according to my notes, but we can double-check with Midge."

"*Midge?*"

"Midge Sarko from *Hotel 9*." He looks around, as if trying to find her, peeking down a hallway, and looking into another room. "She'll be looking after all of you this weekend."

I feel the smile on my face widen. Midge is the psycho chambermaid who collects her victims' fingers in the pockets of her apron.

"I'm not sure where she is, so why don't I show you to your room." He pulls a notepad from his pocket. "You're in room nine."

"Sweet deal," I say, grabbing a couple more cookies.

He leads us through the living room, past a screwed-up ceramic rooster sitting by the fireplace. Its bright yellow eyes must be connected to a motion detector because it crows as I walk by, *almost* making me jump. We head upstairs to room number nine. I step inside, completely jazzed by what I see. There's a drafting table in the corner with an art caddy stocked with pencils, charcoals, and painting stuff. Lining the walls are illustrations from some of my favorite artists, like Haig Demarjian and Virgil Finlay, as well as a few pieces I don't recognize. A poster of Captain Death Row, my favorite band, hangs over the bed. It's an illustration of Captain Death—his smiling skull with a gap between his two front teeth—sporting a bandanna and sunglasses.

There are two beds in the room. I'm tempted to push them together so I can be like Bloody Bathrow, the lead guitarist of the Masochistic Underbellies. I saw Bloody's place on a show called *Crash Pads*. He's got a custom twenty-foot wide bed that he calls his kitty ride.

Beyond the beds, on the far wall, are a bunch of high-end guitars—a couple of them with metallic red and gold paint jobs. I've never tried to play, but maybe Blake thinks that I should. "There's no way you're getting rid of me after just two nights," I say, thinking how jealous my dad would be.

"Shall I leave you to arrange your things?" the driver asks.

I've yet to catch his name and at this point it feels weird to ask. "Solid." I flash him the peace sign and stick out my tongue, Gene Simmons–style. If only it were covered in faux blood.

Once he leaves, I set my sketchbook down on the table and

flop back onto my new bed. It's bigger than my naked mattress at home. Our whole apartment could probably fit into the living room and entryway of this place alone.

I stuff a couple of cookies into my mouth and look up at the ceiling. Another of Haig's illustrations stares back down at me. It's done in dark pastels: cherublike children sleeping peacefully in bed while a sharp-toothed demon with bleeding eyes hovers inches away. It's way cool. And these cookies are way delicious. I think I've died and gone to Dark House heaven.

IVY

"JUST AROUND THIS BEND," THE DRIVER SAYS. "YOU must be anxious to stretch your legs."

I'm anxious, period.

We turn off the main road onto a long dirt path, and finally I'm able to see a house in the distance. As we get closer, I spot a sign over the front door: WELCOME TO THE DARK HOUSE.

"Is this really the B and B?" I ask, feeling my stomach twist. There's no parking lot, not one other car. "Is anyone else staying here?"

He gives me a curious look. "Don't you recognize this place from the Nightmare Elf movies? This house was made to look like the real thing. Aren't you a fan of Justin Blake's work?"

"Of course," I lie, the light finally dawning. The accommodations are movie themed.

I retrieve my bags from the back of the hearse, picturing my parents' caskets—the cherry wood, the engraved crosses, the satin interior lining.

"Welcome to the Dark House!" a voice bellows, pulling me back to earth.

I turn to find a boy standing behind me. He's probably my age, dressed in layers of gray and black. His wavy dark hair is held back with a bandanna, and there are silver hoops pierced through his eyebrow, nostril, and lip.

"Are you one of the winners?" I ask him.

"That depends . . . was Justin Blake born in Knoxville, Tennessee?"

"Maybe?"

"*Errrh*," the boy lets out a game-show buzzer sound, denoting my wrong answer. "The correct response would've been yes. And if you were truly a Justin Blake fan you'd have known where he was born, as well as which schools he attended, and where he now lives. I'm Garth, by the way." He extends his hand for a shake. His fingers are loaded with more sterling silver jewelry than I've ever seen in one place.

"I'm Ivy." I shake his hand, fully aware that my palms are cold and clammy. "I guess you could say that I'm a fairly new fan of Blake's."

Garth closes the rear door of the hearse before moving around to the driver's side window. "I can take things from here," he tells the driver.

As if I couldn't feel more uneasy.

Still, bags in hand, I follow him inside, relieved that it's not creepy like the exterior. A wide open space is furnished with an L-shaped sofa, velvety chairs, and eclectic antiques—an artful blending of color, texture, and style. There's a workstation by the far wall. Beyond it is a set of stairs, and rooms to the right and left. A large granite island separates the living room space from a state-of-the art kitchen so similar to the Spicy Italian Chef's that I almost have to pinch myself. "Is that a real Pompeii oven?" I ask, pointing at it.

Garth sniffs in my direction, evidently too distracted by my smell—the scent of my essential oils maybe—to answer.

"Has anyone else arrived yet?" I ask, my anxiety mounting by the moment.

"Two chicks I've yet to see—one went for a walk, so says Midge, resident watchdog; the other won't open her door . . . at least not for me." He grins, as if the idea of that makes him proud. He leans forward to sniff the side of my face. "Is that A-positive I smell on you?"

"A-positive?" I ask, wondering if that's the name of a new perfume.

"Your blood," he attempts to explain. "It's type A, right?"

I don't know how to respond—or if he's even being serious.

"I'll bet you clot really well, don't you?" He winks. "No coagulation problems for you."

"Welcome!" a woman says, coming down the stairs. She's wearing a maid's uniform—a black dress with a frilly bib apron over it—and there are little-girl ribbons in her hair. "You must be Ivy," she says with a smile. "I was just turning down your bed. I know it's a little early, but I figured you all might be tired. I see that you've met Garth."

Garth appears distracted again. He moves away, down the hall, into another room, slamming the door behind him. The noise makes my insides jump.

"Everything okay?" the woman asks me. Her shimmery white hair matches her pearly teeth and the shadow on her lids. She reminds me of Southern Sally Cooks from the Food Channel.

I manage to nod, trying to get a grip.

"I'm Midge." She smiles wider, exposing a shiny gold tooth. "You need anything, you just call on me. So what do you say . . . Are you ready to check out your room?"

We go upstairs and down a long hallway. The floorboards creak beneath my step. "Here we are," she says, opening the door to room number two.

It's larger than I expected, with two full beds. A giant, life-size cardboard cutout of Julia Child is positioned at the foot of one of them. "Wow," I say, startled by the sight of Julia holding a raw chicken up by its legs.

"I take it that someone's a cooking fan," Midge says.

It's true. I've been cooking pretty intensely since my parents were murdered. Not only is it a distraction, but it also makes me feel in control—wielding knives; the excuse to cut, slice, grate, chop.

"Ivy?" she asks.

I go to take a breath, but the air gets stuck in my chest, deep in my lungs. I sit down on the edge of the bed and silently count to ten, wondering what the hell I'm doing here and what I was even thinking. I touch the aromatherapy pendant around my neck, telling myself to relax. I unplug the cork and close my eyes, breathing in the cedarwood oil, reminding myself of its ability to induce tranquility.

"Do you need some water? Are you not feeling well?"

"I'll be fine," I say, finally able to catch my breath.

"Well, as you can probably guess, the winners' rooms are tailored to each of your individual tastes and interests, based on the personality profiles that you filled out."

I gaze over at the other side of the room. It's Barbie pink and suited for a dancer, with a ballet bar and a rack of dance shoes. A cursive sign over the mirror reads *Dance with Me*. "Is someone else sharing this room?" I ask, spotting a leopard-print suitcase at the foot of the other bed.

"Yes. Taylor. You'll be meeting her soon. She just went out for a walk. It's such a glorious day, isn't it?" Midge opens the drapes wide, letting in the light. It's late afternoon, and the sun's orange glow sinks down through the tree limbs, casting a strip of light over my bed, illuminating a copy of Deena Diddem's latest book, *Dare to Diddem*. (Note: in Deena-speak, *diddem* means to throw together random ingredients from your fridge and pantry and end up with a tasty new dish.)

"Just a little gift from Mr. Blake," Midge says. "I assume you're familiar with Deena's work?"

Deena Diddem, thirty-three years old, born in Toronto, the only child of Chuck and Nancy, climbed the culinary ladder, starting her career in the prepared foods section of her local supermarket. She's now the Food Channel's number one–rated chef.

I take the book and open to a flagged page. Not only has Deena signed the copy, but she's also written me a note.

Dear Ivy,

A little bird told me that you're a big fan of my show. I'm so flattered. Thank you so much!
I also heard that you love to cook. Who knows, maybe one day our paths will cross. In the meantime, keep on diddeming! Best of luck!

Love,
Deena

I run my fingers over her words.

"You like?" Midge asks.

"More like *love*."

"Great." She smiles. "Now if you don't need anything else,

I'll leave you to settle in. You'll notice the itinerary for the week-end on the night table."

"Thanks," I say, reaching to take it, more excited about this weekend than I ever thought possible and more hopeful than ever before.

WEEKEND ITINERARY

FRIDAY

2–7 p.m.	*Dark House Dreamers arrive*
8 p.m.	*Creepy comforts dinner—dining room*
9 p.m.	*Final Cut—theater*
9:30 p.m.	*Ghoulish desserts—dining room*

SATURDAY

10 a.m.–2 p.m.	*A brunch to die for—dining room*
4 p.m.	*Hearse leaves for the set—lobby*

SUNDAY

9 a.m.–noon	*Dead End Brunch for any remaining survivors—dining room*
2 p.m.	*Hearse returns Dark House survivors to the airport—lobby*

PARKER BRADLEY

INT. ENTRYWAY, DARK HOUSE—DAY

ANGLE ON

WOMAN, 50-something, dressed up as Midge Sarko, one of Justin Blake's most villainous characters; a chambermaid from *Hotel 9*, who kills her guests with household items (a turkey timer, a toilet bowl plunger, soap scum remover).

                    MIDGE SARKO
Welcome, you must be Parker.

                         ME
And you're obviously Midge. Anyone
ever tell you that you look just like
Tina Maitland, the actor who played
Midge in the movie?

I move CLOSER on the POCKETS OF HER APRON.
The curly handle of Midge's signature
paring knife sticks out—always ready
to slice off a souvenir finger for her
collection.

                    MIDGE SARKO
                     (winking)
Tina's just an actor. I'm the real
McCoy.

I lower my camera to shake her hand.

                    MIDGE SARKO
Sorry about your flight delay.

                    ME

What's an extra two and a half

hours on the tarmac, right?

                MIDGE SARKO

Well, if it's any consolation, it was

an extra two and a half hours for your

driver too. He was already on his way

to get you by the time he learned of

the delay.

                    ME

Bummer for him.

                MIDGE SARKO

But lucky for us, because you're here

now. Come on, I'll show you to your

room.

I follow Midge through the house, filming the whole way, as the infamous swish-swish sound of her ass fills the loud silence.

"Excited?" she asks.

"Are you kidding? I can hardly believe this is real." I found out about this contest totally by chance doing research for my film class; it was posted on a fan site for Justin Blake, notable horror director/producer/screenwriter. The site was littered with photos of Blake, favorite movie clips, and tons of Nightmare Elf–inspired fan fiction. I'd forgotten what a cult following Blake has. I used to be a fan too, back when I first discovered horror and didn't know much about the genre.

Someone had posted an entry that read: "Want to meet Justin Blake and get a behind-the-scenes look at his new confidential film project? E-mail me: thenightmare.elf@gmail.com."

I sent an e-mail, figuring I wouldn't hear back. But ten minutes later the contest guidelines appeared in my inbox. And eight months later, here I am.

Midge stops in front of the door at the very end of the hall. "This is it."

I point my camera into the room just before mine, wondering where the other winners are, looking for something else interesting to shoot.

ANGLE ON GIRL

GIRL, 18-ish, sits on her bed, looking down at her hands. There's a tiny bottle between her fingers, hanging from a silver chain.

CLOSER ON GIRL'S FACE

Brown eyes, heart-shaped face, long dark
hair. She's way too beautiful to be real.

The girl looks back at me and I'm totally
caught.

"Hey," I say, lowering my camera, suddenly feeling like a
creep. "I was just shooting my arrival."

My explanation sucks, and she knows it too. Her forehead
furrows as she looks toward my camera; it's half-tucked behind
my back, as if I could possibly hide it now.

"Coming?" Midge asks me.

I give the girl an awkward wave and then proceed to my room.
A king-size bed greets me, the cover of which has dozens of hungry, open-mouthed eels scattered across the blue fabric.

"I guess somebody has a sick sense of humor," I say, zooming
in with my camera, remembering the essay I submitted for the
contest.

"How's that?" Midge asks, evidently clueless.

A laptop station sits beyond the bed with one of those ergo-
nomic chairs—one that probably cost more than my car.

"Nice," I say, moving farther inside.

As if on cue, music starts to play. An old black-and-white movie cranks to life on a projector screen on the far wall. The quality of the film is grainy, but I'd recognize this scene anywhere: it's nighttime, there's a storm outside, and an unsuspecting couple falls victim to the classic stranded-car-by-the-side-of-the-road routine. *"The Old Dark House,"* I say. Circa 1932, if I'm remembering correctly from my History of Film course. "How fitting for the weekend."

"Should I assume that things are to your liking?" Midge asks.

"Definitely." I aim my camera at the bookshelves lining the room. They're jammed with screenplays—what has to be at least five hundred of them.

"You'll notice that some of them have been signed," Midge says, following my gaze.

"Signed by whom?" I ask, noticing a copy of *Citizen Kane*, one of my favorite films of all time.

"It varies." She grabs a copy of *The Shawshank Redemption* off the shelf. "Sometimes the writer, sometimes the director. This one's been signed by Morgan Freeman."

"No way." I set my camera down to take a peek.

"Mr. Blake keeps quite a collection." She smiles wide, exposing a shiny gold tooth. "Now, if you'll excuse me, I have some dinner preparations to attend to."

Once she leaves, I continue to check out the screenplays.

Cameron Crowe. Alfred Hitchcock. Stanley Kubrick. John Hughes. It's too good to be real. They don't even know me here, so how can they trust that I won't steal a few?

I grab the script for *The Silence of the Lambs* and then turn to sit on my bed, startled to find that I'm not alone. The girl from next door is standing in my doorway.

"I'm sorry to bother you." Her eyes search my face, as if checking to make sure that I'm okay with her being here.

"No bother at all." I mean, seriously? Holy shit.

"I'm Ivy." Her straight dark hair hangs past her shoulders, over a long purple sundress that stretches to the floor.

"Parker," I say, trying my best not to stare.

But she's not even looking at me now. Her eyes are fixed on the projector screen—on the group of people taking refuge from the storm. They're sitting around the dinner table at the Femm family estate. There's a pounding on the door.

Ivy's eyes widen.

"This is actually a pretty safe scene in the film," I tell her.

"Okay," she says, even though she's totally *not* okay. Her face is completely flushed.

I go to shake her hand, but she's holding her cell phone and we end up making a weird cell phone–hand sandwich.

"Sorry," she says. There's an awkward smile on her face. "I

need to call home, but I can't get reception, and I'm hoping it's just my phone's issue."

"Not just your issue. There's no reception here, at least that's what the hearse guy said, but he also mentioned something about a landline in the living room downstairs."

"Thanks." She smiles. There's an irresistible spray of freckles across her nose and cheeks. "I promised I'd call home when I arrived."

"Where's home?"

"Boston, just north of it. And you?"

"San Diego, just south of it."

"Wow," she says. "We couldn't be farther away from one another."

"Not for the next forty-eight hours we're not." It takes me a beat to realize what I've said—how cheesy it sounds—and my face flashes a thousand degrees of hotness.

Ivy notices, and her smile shifts to a smirk. She must find my embarrassment amusing.

"The last hearse is pulling up," Midge calls. "It must be Shayla and Frankie, the final two Dark House Dreamers."

"Do you want to go down to meet them?" Ivy asks.

Not especially, I think, wondering if she has a boyfriend. But I tell her I'd like to, anyway.

NATALIE

MY ROOM AT THE DARK HOUSE HAS NO MIRRORS. IT was the very first detail I checked. Instead, it's decorated with all-things Justin Blake: T-shirts, key chains, comic books, clapboards, the LEGO-constructed version of Hotel 9, and a collection of Pez dispensers of some of his most notorious characters.

The suit Justin Blake wore to the Oscars in 1999 hangs on a hook, opposite my bed. I reach into one of the pockets and find an old gum wrapper. I sniff the silver packaging. It smells like berries. I run the tip of my tongue over the paper, finally stuffing the entire thing into my mouth. I chew the wrapper down, imagining the gum between his teeth, flipping over his tongue.

I remove the jacket from the hook and slip it over my shoulders, picturing Justin Blake on the red carpet, waving to his fans. I wave too, moving to stand in front of a movie poster for *Night Terrors II*, imagining that I'm his date for the premiere.

The far wall, behind a spare bed, is wallpapered with maps and postcards from around the world. I'm assuming there's some Blake-flavored connection. There's also a director's chair, a rack of men's shoes (size eleven), and an assortment of hairbrushes and combs (perhaps for Blake's thick wavy hair), though I don't spot any residual hair strands.

I check out the chair. It's been signed by Blake. I run my finger over a spot where the ink got smudged. I sit down, feeling overwhelmed and undeserving. Why does someone like me get to be so lucky, when someone like Harris got such a raw deal?

I look toward the closet, wondering if there might be more clothing and collectibles inside. I hurry over and slide open the closet door.

A full-length mirror stares back at me. It takes me a second to realize the reflection on the glass is my own—that it isn't some Nightmare Elf monster.

Was my reflection always this horrible? My face so long? My legs this short? My hands so big? Could my skin be any more pasty?

Others have arrived. I can hear the sound of new voices, the clunking of suitcases, the trampling of feet up and down the stairs.

I whip off the jacket, double-check the lock on the door to my room, and wedge a chair beneath the knob. Sitting on the floor at the foot of my bed, I pull off my wig. There's an eight-strand wad of hair clenched between my fingertips. Who do I think I am to be wearing Justin Blake's jacket? Or chewing his gum wrapper? Sitting in his chair? Thinking about trying on a pair of his shoes?

Even Taylor could tell that I didn't belong here. "Are you going to be okay?" she asked, on our hearse ride from the airport. She didn't even know me. We'd sat on opposite ends of the plane, had only exchanged a few words since we'd landed, but still she could sense that something was off.

"I thought this was what I wanted." I turned away, faced the window, drew a heart on the glass in the steam from my breath. "No one knows I'm here."

"Not even your parents?" she asked.

I could see her reflection in the window glass. Her dark blond hair was pulled back from her face, accentuating her wide green eyes, her pinched nose, and her perfectly pouted lips. Perfectly balanced features.

"I just left," I told her. Packed my bags, called a cab, snatched some money out of my mother's stash in the oatmeal box, and bolted. My mother had told me to be ready by three, that we were going to see a new therapist. I said I'd be waiting. And I wasn't lying: I *was* waiting. My heart pounding, I stood in my bedroom window, gazing out at the street, anticipating who would arrive first—either her or the taxi I called. The winner would dictate my destination. The taxi won, and off I went, on automatic pilot, to the airport, through the check-in, and then onto the plane, shocked that I'd done it. Defied them. Defied Harris. And in such a major way.

"Wow," Taylor said.

I could tell from her tone that she didn't know whether to be happy or sad for me. I didn't know either. This trip wasn't like a secret tattoo that I could hide. There was no turning back, no concealing what I'd done beneath layers of dark clothing.

"We're here," the driver announced as we pulled up in front of the Dark House. "You two are the first to arrive."

Taylor tried to hide her smile with a nibble of her lip. I hated that I was spoiling her excitement. I wanted to be excited too.

Hours later, sitting on the floor, I wonder if Taylor has turned up; it seems she wandered off. Earlier, Midge forced her way into my room to see if Taylor might be hiding somewhere.

I rock back and forth, watching the room in anticipation, as if it might spring to life at any moment—as if I'm in the audience, waiting for the movie of my life to start. I yank the eight-strand wad of hair. The action feeds my blood, soothes my nerves, slows the fleeting thoughts through my head.

My hair strands stick in the creases of my fingers. I sprinkle them over the rug, imagining them like seeds that might one day grow into something healthy.

FRANKIE RICE

ONCE THE PLANE LANDS, THE OLD GUY SITTING NEXT to me spills his pill-meds all over the floor. I should ignore it, but I help him out, exiting the plane a good ten minutes after everybody else.

The silver lining? I'm picked up by a Cadillac hearse. The platinum lining? There's a hot girl sitting inside it.

"Hey," I say, joining her in the backseat.

There's a huge-ass smile on her face, like we're long lost friends and she's been waiting to see me all day. "Hey back at you."

She's cute—*really* cute with insanely bright golden-brown eyes; they're framed behind a pair of square black glasses.

"I'm Shayla," she says, sticking her hand out for a shake. "Shay, for short."

"Frankie," I say, shaking her hand. "No shortening required."

"Too funny." She laughs, despite the lameness of the joke. "Were you on the flight from JFK, because I totally didn't see you? Where are you from . . . and cool bracelet, by the way. Is that a Celtic knot?"

"Yes. Just south of Richmond. And the symbol for infinity, actually."

"As in Justin Blake forever?" She giggles.

"Something like that." I smile. She's so unbelievably perky.

We ride to the place where we're staying, with Shayla chattering on the whole way about art, politics, books she's read, places she's traveled. I try to listen to most of it, but I'm so busy anticipating what it'll be like to meet Justin Blake—how I should act and what I should say—that it's hard to keep up.

Finally we pull up in front of the Dark House B and B. Some lady dressed up as Midge Sarko greets us in the entryway.

"It is *so* nice to meet you," Shayla says, jumping in front of me to shake the woman's hand. "What an incredible opportunity this is."

Other winners are already here. A guy comes forward to shake our hands. "Hey," he says. "I'm Parker."

I introduce myself and Shayla—not that Shayla needs any introduction. She's already pumping Parker for info, asking him where he's from and when he got here, tossing me to the side. "This weekend is going to be *so* super fun," she tells him.

A guy layered in dark clothes and silver jewelry is sitting on a couch. He looks up from his sketchpad as I approach. "Hey, man," he says. "I'm Garth Vader."

"As in Luke Skywalker's father?"

"Garth with a *G*," he says, correcting me, as if the distinction is even worth it. "My dad's a huge Star Wars fan."

"I'm Frankie," I say, extending my hand for a shake. "Where are you from . . . besides the dark side, that is?"

"Delaware," he says, immune to the joke. He sniffs his fingers after shaking my hand. "O-positive, right?"

"Excuse me?"

"It's a gift . . . my ability to sniff out blood type. You're O-positive, aren't you?"

"Cool trick," I say, unfazed to find someone like him here— someone who wears his inner freak on his sleeve. Still, as psycho as he seems, he's right about my blood type.

I peek at his sketchpad. Is it any wonder that he's doing a color sketch of a two-headed ghoul? A mixture of blood and puke spews out of the double mouths, pouring down like rain. The guy may be a walking cliché, but he's actually pretty talented.

"Hey, there," Shayla says, making a beeline in Garth's direction. Clearly this girl has a social agenda. She plops down beside him. "So, let's hear it: What's your story? Who are you and what was your worst-ever nightmare? Holy yum fest," she says, before he can answer anything. The girl is a complete spaz. There's a plateful of Nightmare Elf cookies on the table in front of them. "No wonder it smells like a bakery in here." She takes one, proceeding to tell Garth that she's from the West Village and that the bakery near her apartment is "out-of-this-world fabu-licious."

My gaze travels to a girl in the corner, talking on the phone. She reminds the person on the other end to take their medicine and brush their teeth.

"That's Ivy," Parker says, standing at my side now. "I'm not sure if you noticed it yet, but we don't get cell phone reception here, so if you want to make a call, you have to use the landline."

"No calls for me," I say with a smile. The last thing I want is to listen to my dad whine about how I deserted him with two engine rebuilds and three front axle replacements. "It's nice to have a couple of days off."

"Especially when those days involve a major movie legend, right?"

"Totally." I love that he gets it too.

"Shayla? Frankie?" Midge is standing at the kitchen island, mixing up some sort of green punch drink. "Would you like to see your rooms?"

"Hold on," Shayla says, looking around. "Is everybody here? Are we all the winners?"

"Everybody's arrived," Midge says, dropping a handful of fake black spiders into the punch. "But not everybody's in this room. Taylor, Ivy's roommate, went for a walk and should be returning shortly. And, Shayla, *your* roommate is already upstairs."

"And I haven't even met her yet?" Shayla springs up from the couch—this is obviously a national emergency. If she were only half as cute, her eternally perky demeanor might be annoying.

We follow Midge upstairs, but the door to Shayla's room is locked. "Natalie?" Midge raps lightly on the door.

Meanwhile, Shayla continues to chatter on, saying how pumped she is to meet her roommate, like this is the most exciting thing on earth. And I suppose it is. I mean, I'm pretty stoked too. And it's sort of cool to be with people who share that same vibe, rather than at the garage where everything is always a downer, where doom and gloom are as encouraged as cash payments.

"Do you need some help?" I ask, watching as Midge struggles with the key.

"The lock already turned," Midge says, "so I'm pretty sure the key works."

"In other words, the door is stuck?" Shayla asks.

"Natalie?" Midge calls again. "Can you open up? Your roommate is here and she'd really like to meet you."

"Maybe she's sleeping," Shayla says.

Midge frowns, like someone just stole from her collection of severed fingers.

"Let me try," I say.

Midge steps to the side, and I grab the knob, forcing my weight against the door. It doesn't budge. "There must be something propped up beneath the knob, on the inside." I take a step back to gain momentum and then lunge at the door. At the same moment, the door opens and I go flying inside, barely catching myself from falling on my ass.

A girl stands there. Black hair, dark clothing. Way too Goth for my taste, but you can tell that she'd be totally hot with her full lips and slanted blue eyes—that is if she'd stop shopping at Freaks "R" Us.

"Sorry," Natalie says. She tries to smile, even though it looks like she's been crying. Her skin is blotchy and her eyes are red.

This is way too much drama for me, so I ask Midge to point

me in the direction of my room. She nods to an open door, across the hall—room number nine.

There are two beds inside. I'm assuming mine's the one without all the crap—the heap of clothes and art supplies, not to mention the bloody skeleton poster hanging above the headboard. I recognize the skeleton. It's from the album cover of a heavy metal band from the '80s. The lead guitarist plays a Gibson Explorer.

I move to my half of the room, noticing six guitars set up on the far wall. There's a signature Eric Clapton Fender Stratocaster, signed by the man himself. There's also a Telecaster signed by Jim Root from Slipknot. "Holy shit," I say, under my breath. These must be worth a fortune.

Still keeping my eye on the Clapton, I venture to touch a '70s Black Beauty Les Paul Custom—the same model that Peter Frampton made famous with his album *Frampton Comes Alive*. The thing is an absolute stunner with its sleek black body and mother-of-pearl block inlays.

I reach for a Gretsch, beyond stoked to see that it's signed by Jack White from the White Stripes. Seriously, do I need to pinch myself?

"What color is your blood?"

I turn to find Garth there. This is his room too. "Man, you scared the crap out of me."

"What color is your blood?" he repeats.

"I'm pretty sure it's red, the last time I checked. Hey, are these your guitars, or do you know where they came from?"

"*Do* you check?" he persists. There's a screwed-up smile on his face, like he just ate his family for lunch. "Do you cut your skin open and watch the blood leak out?"

"Not lately."

"You do know that blood is actually blue, right? When it's inside the body, running through the veins. It isn't until you cut yourself open and the blood hits the air that it turns that red color."

"Except I'm pretty sure that's a myth," I say, thanks to Ms. Matthews, my science teacher back in middle school. This whole conversation feels pretty middle school, but I play along, trying to keep the peace. "The blue color you see in your veins, under the skin, is really just a darker red," I tell him.

"What do you say we put that theory to the test?" He wields his mighty pinky ring; there's an arrow point at the very end— one that could probably do some damage.

Out of the corner of my eye, I spot what appears to be an animal skeleton of some sort on the drafting table by the window.

"Like it?" he asks, following my gaze. His eerie smile grows wider.

I look away, unwilling to let his bullshit get the best of me, and resume checking out the guitars.

"It belongs to a squirrel that pissed me off," he continues. "Now, it's a source of artistic inspiration. My good luck charm. Would you believe that I got stopped in the airport for carrying it? Security questioned me for over an hour. They went through all my bags and asked me if I've ever had thoughts of hurting others. I missed my connecting flight because of them. I was supposed to have traveled with Natalie and Taylor . . . both of whom I've yet to meet, by the way."

"And I should give a shit about any of this, because . . ." I turn to look at him again. He may be super tall, but I can tell that I'm at least twice his size—that beneath all those layers of gray, there's the body of a scrawny seven-year-old kid.

A second later, there's a knock at the open door, interrupting us.

Parker's there. "Hey, you guys want to come check something out?"

"Absolutely," I say, returning the Gretsch to the rack, more than eager to ditch this freak.

SHAYLA

THE BOYS HERE ARE SUPER CUTE, AND I'M SUPER excited to get to know them more—to get to know *everybody* more—but my roommate is a buzzkill.

"I want to go home," Natalie says, sulking at the edge of her bed, her cell phone clenched in her hand.

"Nonsense," Midge tells her. "You're just tired and probably hungry, but that's nothing that some rest and a warm meal wouldn't cure."

"Try clicking your heels together three times," I joke.

But Natalie's not really the joking type. She stares down at her clunky black boots (for the record, Dr. Martens originals). I feel kind of sorry for her—and not because of her lack of style, though that's pity rendering too. Having spent the last nine years at four different boarding schools, I've had my fair share of abrupt transitions and seen some nasty cases of homesickness. My best friend Dara's included.

"Maybe you could just give us a moment," I tell Midge.

"Sure," she says, but she seems unsure, as if Natalie is a delicate flower that I could trample with one wrong step. Thankfully, Midge leaves us alone anyway.

I sit down beside Natalie on the bed, noticing that her hair looks even gnarlier than mine does, *pre*-relaxer. It's like something straight out of a Tim Burton movie—big and dark and creepy and fake. I try to imagine how she might look if she'd fix her hair and shed the bag-lady clothing. I'd bet she'd be really striking. She has a model's facial bone structure: high cheekbones, a nose that turns slightly upward, and a perfectly pointed chin. Plus, her lips look naturally full and her skin appears virtually flaw- and pore-less.

"So, Miss Natalie, where are you from? And what do you like?"

"I actually prefer to be called Nat."

"As in the bloodsucking insect? News flash, bloodsucking is so five years ago," I say, still trying to keep things light.

"You don't have to babysit me, you know."

"I think roommate-sit would be the more accurate term, don't you?" I smile. "Now, tell me, what's with the dark cloud hovering over your sunny time here?"

She gets up and fishes inside her suitcase, pulling out a package of Twizzlers. "I just really miss Harris."

"Your boyfriend?"

"My brother. We're twins."

I can feel the bewilderment on my face, unable to imagine missing my booger-picking brother after five months, never mind five hours. "Well, you could call him, you know . . . on the landline."

"He doesn't want to talk to me."

"Why not?"

She opens the licorice package, twists a stick around her index finger, and gnaws on it like a baby with a teething ring. "I didn't tell him I was coming here. I didn't tell anyone, for that matter."

"So, your parents don't know where you are?"

"They probably have some idea. I mean, they know I won the contest. They just didn't want me to come. Harris didn't either." She swallows a mouthful of licorice before loading her fingers with a couple more sticks.

"*I* could call them," I offer, suddenly remembering that I promised my mom that I'd call her, too. I flop back onto the bed and kick up my legs, admiring my checkerboard pedicure. "Not to brag or anything, but I *do* have a way with parents. It's one of my hidden talents."

"I don't think so."

"Are you sure?" I ask, making the checkerboards dance.

A second later, there's a knock on the open door.

It's Parker . . . looking even more amazing than he did ten minutes ago. If I didn't know better, I'd say he just stepped off the runway. I mean, holy hunk of hotness with his broad shoulders, tousled blond hair, chiseled features, and sea glass–worthy blue eyes.

"Come on," he says. "We're all next door, in Ivy and Taylor's room. There's something you'll want to see." There's a delicious grin on his face. He's just so incredibly yummy.

"Totally," I say, jumping up from the bed. But then I look back at Natalie.

She's turned away now, silently asserting a big fat no.

It's all I can do not to scream. "Just give us a few minutes, okay?" I tell Parker, faking a smile, and closing the door behind him.

"You should go," Natalie says, between bites of licorice.

"Why don't you come too? I mean, we're here to get to know everyone, *right*?" I spend the next eleven minutes telling her about my arrival at Winston Academy, the only black girl in a sea of fair-skinned blondes with names like Josie, Bunny, Kiki, and Coco. "But I had to eventually mix in and give people a chance. I couldn't just sit around sulking in my room all day."

Still, bag of candy in hand, Natalie moves to lie down on her bed, drawing the covers over her face.

I suppose I can take a hint. I leave her alone and hop next door. But, to my surprise, no one's in there now. I go inside, curious to know what Parker was talking about—what I so desperately needed to see.

Half of the room is decorated with cookbooks and food videos, not to mention a creepy cutout of Julia Child holding a slimy chicken carcass. *Classy.* The other half is baby-doll pink and suited to a dancer. I wonder which side is Ivy's.

I continue to look around, checking to see if anything appears off, finally spotting a rack of ballet slippers. They're all so pretty and delicate—like tiny works of art. Even though I'm not a dancer now, I used to take ballet when I was a kid—back when it was okay for little-girl ballerinas to be something other than white and emaciated. But sometime around the age of eleven, when I started to sprout boobs and booty, and when I decided to trade my frizz-ball hair bun for neat little cornrows, my ballet teacher suggested that my "look" and body type might be better suited to hip-hop, which totally squelched my dreams of being in *Swan Lake* one day. I haven't danced since, which Dara always thought was crazy. "You're an incredible dancer," she used to say. "Don't let someone else's opinion dictate your life."

If only Dara had taken her own advice.

I peer over my shoulder to make sure that no one's looking, and then I go to try on a shimmering white slipper, but I can barely squish my toes in, confirming what my ballet teacher was talking about: some of us simply don't fit.

I move over to the closet, noticing a stash of glittery costumes, hoping that there's one for Princess Odette, my favorite character from *Swan Lake*. I search the racks, eager to find one before someone comes in and sees me here.

There are costumes from *The Nutcracker*, *A Midsummer Night's Dream*, *Peter Pan*, and *Sleeping Beauty*, but I don't see any for *Swan Lake*. I take some *Nutcracker* wings, imagining myself as the Sugar Plum Fairy.

Then I spot something else. At the back of the closet. A streak of red on the wall.

I part the costumes to get a better look. Dark letters on the back of the closet spell out GET OUT BEFORE IT'S TOO LATE.

GARTH

"OKAY, WHO HAS THE SICK SENSE OF HUMOR?" SOMEONE shouts.

"Sounds like somebody's looking for me," I holler back, proceding down the hallway, wielding my mighty ax.

It was Shayla's voice. She's in Ivy and Taylor's room. There's a sexy little smirk on her face. "Did *you* do this?" She points inside a closet.

Before I can ask or see what she's talking about, the others come back upstairs. I swing the ax, picturing myself as Sidney Scarcella in *Hotel 9: Blocked Rooms* in the lobby scene, when poor

Mrs. Teetlebaum ventures from her room in the middle of the night. But they're all so busy blathering on that they don't even notice.

"Ohmygosh," Shayla bursts out as soon as she sees Parker. "So, I was just checking out the costumes, and . . . wait, where did you get that?" She's looking at me now, referring to my ax. A curious smile sits on her lips. I can tell she wants to play too.

"In the bathroom. The blade was stuck in the wall—just a sweet little reminder of why we're all here."

"Is it real?" Ivy asks.

"Unfortunately, no." I sigh, scratching my head with the plastic blade. "But it's the thought that counts, right?"

I move into the room and take a peek inside the closet. The costumes are pushed to the side, exposing the back wall. "Get out before it's too late," I say, reading the flaming-red words. I let out a big fat yawn. "I mean, seriously, this is *it*?"

"Did *you* do it?" Parker asks me.

"If only I could take the credit." I step closer to examine the writing. Some of the letters have fingerprints in the individual strokes. But, I know my stuff. "It wasn't written in blood," I say, "in case that was a concern."

"This from the guy who thinks that blood is as blue as his balls," Frankie says.

"I don't really believe that blood is blue. I just wanted to see if

I could convince *you* that it was." I smile, making sure to expose my pointy incisors, hoping to psych him out. "If this were *real* blood there would be droplets all over the floor. Plus, if it's been at least an hour since this was written—and I'm assuming it has—the blood would've had time to oxidize."

"Meaning?" Parker asks.

"Meaning, it would've browned by now. It's got to be paint or marker, or something else—a nifty corn syrup concoction, maybe." I lean in to give the writing a sniff, noticing a slightly glossy sheen. "It's still wet."

"So, I guess that rules out the theory that it was done by a former guest," Shayla says.

It's lip gloss. I'm sure of it. I can tell from the beeswax scent. I reach out to touch the stain. "On second thought, maybe it *is* blood," I lie, pretending to lick the smear from my finger.

Ivy lets out a shriek. She's way too easy to disturb. My dad would be all over her paranoid ass, injecting fake blood into her toothpaste tube, and other "fun" stuff like that.

"Oh my God! Remember that scene in *Hotel 9: Enjoy Your Stay*?" Shayla asks. "When Emma Corwin commits suicide out of self defense?"

"So that the killer won't get her." Frankie nods.

"After Emma slits her wrist, she dips her fingers into her own blood and starts to write the word *help* on the window glass," I continue.

"Only she doesn't get past the letter *L*," Shayla says, finishing my thought. Her amber eyes grow wide. There's a certain smart-girl sexiness about her. Maybe it's the square black glasses. Or maybe it's the curvy situation she's got going on beneath that ridiculous housewife tracksuit.

"What if Taylor left us that message?" Ivy asks, still freaking out.

"You seriously need to be medicated," I say. "I mean, think about it: a bunch of Justin Blake horror junkies travel from all over the country to partake in a scary weekend. This sort of stuff is to be expected."

"Okay, but if it was only done in fun, then why hide it in a closet?" Ivy nags. "Why not put it out in the open? This message was done in secret. Maybe Taylor was hiding when she did it."

"Or maybe Taylor doesn't even exist," Frankie says. "What if this whole scenario was created just for our entertainment?"

"There's a movie like that," I say. "Name that film: a group of seemingly random kids gets invited to spend the night in a mansion that's rumored to be haunted, only, in the end, there's nothing random about how the kids were chosen. They were all handpicked according to their personality profiles—sort of like the personality profile that we all had to submit for this contest—and the entire evening of horrors was orchestrated by the hosts."

Despite the accurate description, their faces remain blank.

"It came out in 1997," I continue, giving them a hint. "It bombed at the box office during its debut weekend, but then hit a grand slam in video. Jeffrey Salter was the executive producer, two no-name actors played the leads, and the director was . . ." I hum out the theme song to *Jeopardy*, waiting for someone to reply.

"Errrh," I say, sounding the buzzer.

"Are you talking about *House of Red*?" Parker asks. "Because that actually came out in ninety-six, not ninety-seven. And it was directed by Henri Maltide and *co*-produced by Salter. Maltide was also listed as a producer."

"Okay, but Salter did all the work," I say, correcting him. "Including writing the screenplay, so let's give credit where credit is due, shall we? Oh, and PS, Taylor *is* real, or at least according to Midge she is. She was supposed to be on my connecting flight, along with Natalie, but I got bumped thanks to my pet, Squirrely."

"I'm not even going to ask," Parker says, grabbing his cell phone. He takes a few pictures of the writing.

"Peek-a-boo," Midge sings, poking her head inside the room.

"Was someone looking for me a few minutes ago? I was down in the basement and thought I heard someone call out my name."

Parker points to the bogus message. "We wanted to show you something."

A twinge of surprise forms on Midge's face, but then her expression morphs into a sheepish grin. "Beats me," she says, reaching into the pocket of her apron. She pulls out a handful of bloody fingers. They look eerily realistic, complete with dirty fingernails and hairy knuckles. She holds them out for show and then pops them into her mouth.

This woman is my new idol.

Ivy lets out a gasp, covering her mouth.

"Oh, I'm sorry," Midge says. "How rude of me. Would any-one like a juicy thumb?"

"I would," I tell her.

Midge fishes a hairless thumb from her pocket and hands it to me. I pop it into my mouth. It's bubble gum.

"Are you all hungry?" Midge asks. "Dinner's almost ready."

"Shouldn't we wait for Taylor to get back from her walk?" Ivy asks.

"Taylor phoned just a little while ago, while I was on another call," Midge explains. "She stopped at a diner on Highway 9."

"Is Highway 9 far from here?" Ivy asks.

"*Everything* is far from here." Frankie laughs.

"We already have a car out looking for her," Midge says. "So don't worry. Just come down to the dining room in fifteen minutes. I'll have everything ready."

"Sounds great." I blow out a bubble and pop it with my ax, more than eager to get this party started.

Once Midge and the others file out of the room, only Ivy and I remain. Ivy paces back and forth, completely lost in her own little world, not even noticing the fact that I'm lounging on her bed right now. Part of me almost feels sorry for her—I used to get scared like that too.

I take a deep breath, thinking back to the day my dad pulled me aside and taught me all about Leatherface. "Do you want me to teach you what I know?"

She looks at me, alarm on her face, as if surprised to find me still here.

"About the blood," I explain.

Still no answer.

"Blink once for yes, twice for no," I continue.

She blinks once—on purpose or by accident, I'm not quite sure—and so I get up and stand in front of the closet. "See the glossy sheen?" I say, pointing to the individual letters.

Ivy finally shows a pulse and comes over to join me.

"Now, get real close," I tell her. "Do you smell the beeswax? I think there might also be a hint of petroleum jelly."

"Are you a bloodhound?"

"It's my superpower," I say, only half kidding. I may not be able to detect blood type for real, but ever since I was little, I've had a keen sense of smell—sometimes *so* keen that it became somewhat of a handicap, forever distracting my attention. I failed freshman Bio because Mr. Bing reeked of mothballs. "Do you smell the artificial ingredients?" I ask her.

She shakes her head.

I lean in to sniff the letters again, and that's when I notice it.

"What?" Ivy asks, able to spot the confusion on my face.

I look around the closet, searching for the source, spotting a palm-size smear of blood in the corner, by the floor. I kneel down to check it out. It's had time to oxidize, but I can tell it's still fresh.

"*What?*" Ivy repeats.

"Just more of the lip gloss," I lie, sparing her the truth. It's probably just a fluke thing anyway.

IVY

THE DINING ROOM OF THE DARK HOUSE IS STRAIGHT from a magazine: plum-purple walls, velvet drapes, gold-framed paintings, and a mosaic-tiled floor. Parker's filming the space, doing a close-up of a portrait of a half woman/half feline dressed in a fur coat.

I sit with the others around a marble table lined with thick red candles. Parker takes a seat beside me and bumps his shoulder against mine.

"Everything cool?" he asks, probably noticing that I've been mute for the past several minutes.

Little does he know that there's a ball of tension wedged beneath my ribs, making it hard to breathe. "It's fine," I say, forcing a smile, wanting to prove to myself that I can do this. Getting scared is part of the process, I repeat inside my head, hoping the repetition will make it okay.

A crystal chandelier hangs down from a vaulted ceiling, illuminating our meal, which is kept hidden beneath silver dome covers. Midge lifts the covers, unveiling some of America's most popular comfort foods: mashed potatoes, mac and cheese, green bean casserole, fried chicken, and barbecue spareribs.

"Holy yum-ness," Shayla says. "This is totally the meal from *Nightmare Elf III: Lights Out.* Remember when that couple ran out of gas en route home from their road trip? They went to the Dark House for help, and the family that was staying there at the time—"

"The Kramer family," Garth says to clarify.

"—served this very same meal." Shayla spoons a mound of mashed potatoes onto her plate and then tops it off with a drizzle of gravy.

"Can I pass you something?" Parker asks me.

"I'm good," I say, taking a glob of mac and cheese, even though the thought of ingesting anything right now makes me feel sick.

"So, when do we get to meet Justin Blake?" Frankie asks, as Midge fills our water glasses.

"Tomorrow," she says. "Didn't you find the itinerary in your room?"

"I think I might've been too distracted by the Clapton Fender Stratocaster."

"Nothing but the best for our Dark House Dreamers." She sets a dinner bell in the center of the table. "If anyone needs anything, just give this here a jingle, okay?"

We thank her and she leaves the room, dimming the overhead lights as she goes.

"I have an idea." Shayla perks up in her seat. "How about after dinner we play an icebreaker game. Something to help us get to know one another."

I look over at Natalie, feeling bad that we haven't officially met. "I'm Ivy," I say, somewhat encouraged by her presence—that there might actually be someone here who's more freaked out than me.

The others introduce themselves as well. Natalie flashes a polite smile and then resumes eating her food in silence.

"How about we play spin the bottle?" Garth says, between bites of barbecue spareribs. He flashes us a grotesque smile, his teeth and lips thoroughly saturated with dark red goo.

Shayla laughs in response, making me wonder if there isn't anything she doesn't find hilarious. "How about a Justin Blake trivia game?"

"Except I'd beat all of you in the first round," Garth says.

"Don't be so sure about that one. What year did Blake graduate from college?" Parker asks.

"He didn't graduate," Frankie says. "He never made it through sophomore year."

"No, but he did graduate from Wentley Vocational-Technical School," Garth says. "His father wanted him to become an electrician."

"That actually isn't right," Natalie says, peeking up from her chicken leg. "His father wanted him to become a doctor, but they ended up compromising on electrical work, and that was only because Blake's uncle was a master electrician, so Blake was pretty much guaranteed a job."

Garth pauses from licking his goo-covered fingers. His mouth hangs open, exposing a hunk of chewed up pork. "Holy crap. She speaks."

"She just doesn't speak *to you*," Frankie jokes.

I angle myself in Natalie's direction. "Were you and Taylor on the same flight here? Did you ride in the same car?"

"Yes," she says, poking a hole in the nonexistence theory. "Why?"

"Because Taylor is missing," I tell her.

"Not missing, just not *here*." Garth rolls his eyes.

"I know what we should play," Shayla says, snagging the

conversation back. "How about a game of two truths and a lie?"

"I vote that we don't play any games," Frankie says. "Let's just talk like normal people."

"If only we *were* normal people," Garth says, baring his sauce-smothered teeth once again.

"What did everyone write about for the contest?" Parker asks.

The table goes quiet for several seconds until Frankie ventures to speak. "I wrote about the nightmares I had after my uncle died—about digging his body up and getting trapped underground, right along with him."

"There's a movie like that," Garth says. "About a guy who gets buried alive."

"There are at least *ten* movies like that," Parker says, correcting him. "The idea is actually sort of cliché."

"Were you and your uncle super close?" Shayla asks, turning to Frankie.

"Close enough, I guess," he says. "But it was seeing the burial that *really* messed me up . . . seeing his body lowered into the ground and planted inside the earth, like it could one day grow back to life. What made it worse was that my mom had left a few months before."

"*Left?*" Shayla asks.

"Yep." He nods, drawing a train track across his mound of

mashed potatoes. "She packed her bags and never looked back. This was her bracelet, by the way." He flashes us a gold link chain around his wrist. "It was passed down to her by her father—my grandfather. And, one day, she took it off, fastened it around my wrist, and told me that I could keep it and that we'd always be together."

"The symbol for infinity," I say, spotting the elongated figure eight.

"Which is actually pretty ironic, considering that she took off that following week. Anyway, my dad hates that I wear it—says it's a complete slap in his face—which is why I got this." He lifts the sleeve of his T-shirt. *Rice & Sons* is tattooed on his bicep. "It's the name of my dad's auto repair shop. My brothers have the same one—proof of our loyalty. Needless to say, allegiance is pretty big in my family."

"*I* have tattoos," Natalie says.

"*Plural?*" Garth asks, his eyebrow raised. He gives her body a once over, but only her face and fingers are bare. "How many, where, and of what?"

"Seven. All over. And all for Justin Blake," she says. "I guess I have my allegiances too."

"To a man you've never met?" I ask, genuinely curious about her motivation.

"Is that somehow less acceptable than getting permanently

109

inked to show a supposed loyalty to something that you don't even care about?" Frankie asks, obviously referring to his father's business. "Something that you kind of even resent?"

"You don't *really* have tattoos, do you?" Garth says, zeroed in on Natalie.

"Why would I lie?" she asks.

"I guess there's only one way to prove it." The menacing grin on Garth's face reminds me of the Grinch's after having just stolen Christmas.

"She doesn't need to prove anything to you," Frankie tells him.

Natalie looks at Frankie and a tiny smile crosses her lips. A second later, the lights flicker and go out, tightening the knot in my gut.

"It's just a scare tactic," Parker says. He nods toward the hallway, where the lights are still on. "I'm sure this weekend is going to be full of them."

As if on cue, his words are followed by the roar of thunder—a hard, heavy rumble that reverberates in my bones. Even Shayla jumps at the sound.

I focus on one of the candles, trying to exhale my mounting anxiety, but my breath gets caught in my chest, and I let out a wheeze.

"Are you okay?" Parker asks, placing his hand on my shoulder.

My heart beats fast. My hands start to sweat. I can't seem to get enough air. "I need to go lie down for a bit," I try to say, but the words come out choppy.

"Seriously?" Garth asks. "You're one of the chosen, here for the party. Stay for the rolling credits, why don't you?"

I really wish I could, but right now I need to get away.

PARKER

I WAIT ALL OF FIVE MINUTES BEFORE GOING UPSTAIRS to check on Ivy. "Hello," I call, rapping lightly on the door.

She opens it. Her hair's pulled back. There's a thin veil of sweat over her forehead and neck. Somehow it makes her skin glisten. The bottle pendant that hangs around her neck dangles toward her cleavage.

I nod at the travel mug she's holding. "You got something strong in there?"

"It's chamomile." She smiles. "Want some?" She points to a tin full of tea packets.

"I've got all sorts of flavors and colors: red, green, black, gray, kombucha, oolong, dandelion . . ."

"Thanks," I say, stepping inside her room. "But I'm not much of a tea drinker."

"Really?" She gives me a surprised look, as if not drinking tea is as peculiar as bringing a stash of it along on vacation. She sits down on Taylor's bed and the vee of her dress opens ever so slightly, exposing three solid inches of plump ivory skin. "I'm sorry I freaked out down there."

"Don't apologize. I get it. Being here is making you a wee bit anxious."

"More like a huge bit."

"I mean, I know the message in the closet upset you, and that Taylor's absence really bothers you."

She angles toward the closet and her dress opens up even more. "The message is probably like Garth said—a scare tactic." She looks back at me, straight into my face. "Are you okay? Because if you want to talk about something else, I totally get it."

"Right," I say, but I have no idea what I'm agreeing to, and the confused look in Ivy's eyes tells me that she doesn't know either.

I mentally splash some water onto my face, noticing that she smells intoxicating—like lavender and chamomile. I take a deep breath, trying to picture this whole scene like a movie—*anything* to help keep myself focused.

INT. BEDROOM—NIGHT

One half of the room is decorated for a
dancer, with ballet slippers and costumes;
the other half is full of cookbooks. There
are two full beds.

IVY, 18-ish and unbelievably cute, sits on
one of the beds, wearing a dress that's
driving me crazy.

I move to sit beside her.

                    IVY
        Taylor already started unpacking
        her stuff.

She motions to Taylor's leopard-print
suitcase at the foot of the bed. It's
unzipped. And the top drawer to Taylor's
dresser is only half-closed.

                    ME
        And?

                          IVY

And why would she start unpacking
if she were just going to bolt? I
mean, I suppose I get it. Maybe she
needed some fresh air and wanted to
regroup, which is totally understand-
able. I mean, I keep having to
remind myself what *I'm* still doing
here, and why I even came to begin
with.

                          ME

Why *did* you come?

                          IVY

Why did *you*?

                          ME

For the networking possibilities.
I want to be a filmmaker one
day.

                          IVY

Which explains the video camera.

                    ME

               (nodding)

I only end up using about five
percent of the footage. But still,
getting in the habit of filming
stuff—trying to get those perfect
angles—and then editing clips
together to tell a story . . .
all of that helps make me a better
filmmaker.

                    IVY

Sounds like you really love it.

                    ME

I do. And getting to meet Justin
Blake is a major step in the right
direction. Now, your turn.

                    IVY

I don't know.
               (a shrug)
I guess I entered this contest because
I really love horror.

                    ME

Right.

                    (a smirk)

I should've known that from your
expression during *The Old Dark House*
movie. I think it looked something
like this.

I flash her my most frightful face, my eyes
wide and my mouth arched open in terror.

                    IVY

That obvious, huh?

                    ME

Do you want to be an actress?

                    IVY

Apparently I'm not a very good one if
you're onto me already. Can you keep a
secret? I hate horror. Like, I *really*
hate it. I don't get what the appeal
is . . . why someone would ever want
to be scared.

                              ME

Okay, so it makes *perfect* sense why
you'd want to enter this contest.

                              IVY

Really?

                              ME

Not really. (a grin) How did you even
find out about the contest?

                              IVY

The Nightmare Elf kept e-mailing me.
For whatever reason, despite many
attempts to unsubscribe, I'm on his
e-newsletter list, which means I'm
constantly getting updates about his
numerous contests.

                              ME

Does the Nightmare Elf even *have* an
e-newsletter?

Ivy lets out an exhausted sigh and then flops back onto the bed,
making it impossible for me to stay focused. I put my mental

video camera away, zeroing in on the silhouette of her body beneath the thin cotton sundress—her curvy hips, her narrow waist, and the soft mounds of her chest. It's almost too much to handle, and I don't quite know where to look.

"Ivy?" I ask, after several awkward seconds.

Her eyes are wide. She stares toward the open window. Her chest moves up and down with each breath, accentuating the sweet layer of perspiration on her skin. "What?" she asks, rolling onto her side to face me.

But I've suddenly forgotten the question.

She props herself up on her elbow, brushing up against something beneath the coverlet, by the pillow.

"What is it?" I move closer to get a better look.

Ivy pulls a cell phone from beneath the bedsheet. Like Taylor's luggage, the case is leopard print too.

"I assume that belongs to Taylor?" I ask.

Ivy's mouth falls open. "Why would she go for a walk and not take her cell phone with her?"

"Maybe she forgot it. I forget my cell all the time."

"Yes, but Midge said that Taylor called her."

"She probably used a pay phone."

"I think we should tell the others," she says.

"And *I* think you need to relax. Do you want some more tea?"

Instead of answering, she pockets the cell phone and goes for the door, leaving me even more curious about her.

Natalie

IT'S JUST AFTER DINNER, AND WHILE SHAYLA, GARTH, and Frankie snoop around in the living room, I hang back in the doorway, staring at the phone on the desk.

"Come on," Shayla calls out to Garth, pointing inside a media cabinet.

Meanwhile Frankie checks out a photo album. "Anyone want to see a picture of Blake at prom?"

They continue to look around. And then Shayla moves into the adjoining kitchen, where she lets out a screech.

Frankie drops the album to go see what happened. I move closer too, leaning over the kitchen island.

Shayla whimpers, like she's injured. There's something dark and hairy in her arms. Its body coils against her skin.

"I'm bleeding," she whines.

"Help her!" I cry out.

Frankie tries to assess the situation, but Shayla's crouched on the floor now, her body angled away from him. Garth steps closer and pushes Frankie out of the way. He grabs Shayla, pulls her up, spins her around, and finally we're able to see.

A rat.

A huge, hairy rat.

Its teeth are crusted red. Its mouth opens and closes. "Eek!" it screeches. Or rather, Shayla screeches.

I realize then it's a puppet—the most realistic rat puppet I've ever seen. Shayla's hand is poked into the belly, making the mouth gape open.

"Are you kidding?" Garth laughs. "Where did you find that?"

"In the sink, next to the bloody rubber arm sticking out from the disposal. And, yes, obviously I *am* kidding—kidding you, that is." Her eyes are teary with laughter.

"Payback," Frankie declares. "That's what this calls for, so you'd better watch your back."

"I guess three summers at performing arts camp paid off," she says.

Frankie grabs the rat and chases Shayla with it, making like it's going to bite her. Garth joins in too. He plucks the bloody arm from the sink, following right after them—out of the kitchen and into another room.

Leaving me alone.

I look back at the phone, and then take a seat at the desk. I start to dial, feeling the urge to pull just a few hairs at the nape of my neck. But I push the last digit before I do.

The number connects. I listen to the phone ring, picturing the receiver on the night table in my parents' room, sitting beneath my younger sister Margie's oil painting of Mom. The painting was a surprise portrait, done from Mom's high school graduation photo, and presented to my mother at the town art show, at which Margie won honorable mention and Mom dissolved into a puddle of jubilant tears.

The phone continues to ring. My head is about to explode. I can hear the rush of blood in my ears, making my temples throb.

Finally someone picks up. I hear a click. But no one says a word.

"Hello?" I say, gripping the phone tight. "Mom? Is that you? It's me. Natalie."

I can tell that someone's there. I hear a sniff and then a sigh.

"Mom?" I ask again, figuring that it's her, ever obedient, forever subservient. My name should really be Apple, and hers should be Tree.

"I'm in Minnesota," I say into the receiver. "I took that trip . . .

the contest one that I was telling you about . . . the one where I get to meet Justin Blake. Anyway, I know that you're probably upset, but . . ." My voice trails off. I can't finish the thought. Tears streak down my face.

"Just know that this trip—my going, I mean," I continue, "has nothing to do with you and everything to do with me. I didn't feel like I could give up this opportunity. Justin Blake has been a major part of my life, and I want to tell him—need to tell him, *personally*—how much his work has meant to me."

The truth: it's been my saving grace.

The first time my father told me that I was an accident, I wrote Harris's name all over my body with a ball-point pen— 311 times—convinced that his name would shield me from my father's words.

I went out into the street like that, wearing shorts and a tank. The neighborhood kids didn't know how to respond to me. Mrs. Watson asked if I was feeling all right.

"She's feeling just fine," my dad said, running out to get me. "Just kid stuff." He rolled his eyes, as if she could identify with him. And then he yanked me inside, dragged me into the bathtub, started the water, and threw a bar of soap at my head. "You're not worthy of having Harris's name on you," he said.

I was ten years old; it was the year I discovered the *Nightmare Elf* and *Hotel 9* series.

A couple of years later, when I overheard my parents telling Margie how much they wished I was more like her, I found *Halls of Horror* and its prequel *Forest of Fright*.

Last summer, when the Riskins invited us to their daughter's lavish graduation party, I overheard my mother telling Mrs. Riskin that we'd all love to go. "But Natalie won't be able to make it," she added. "She'll be at sleepaway camp that weekend."

I didn't have sleepaway camp, but thank God I had the *Night Terrors* trilogy.

"Please, say something," I plead. "Tell me that you don't hate me."

I wait for several seconds, but still no one speaks, which makes a bubble form in my throat. It bursts out through my mouth, and I let out a thirsting cry.

"Natalie?" Ivy asks.

She's standing in the doorway. I wonder how long she's been there and how much she already heard.

"What happened?" she asks.

I close my eyes, picturing myself like a piece of paper inside a fire, getting lapped up by the flames, melted away in the heat. But then I realize: the phone's still pressed against my ear. The line's still connected. I never hung up.

Ivy comes and sits beside me. She takes the receiver and places it up to her ear. "Hello?" she asks. "Is someone there?"

Her face furrows, like she doesn't quite understand.

"What?" I ask, desperate to know if it's really my mom.

"They hung up," she whispers. "I heard the phone go click. That doesn't make any sense."

It actually makes perfect sense to me. What I've done—coming here against my parents' wishes—is unforgiveable to them. As angry as they've ever been at me, they've never completely shut me out. "I wish I could talk to Harris."

"And Harris is . . ."

"Huh?" I say, suddenly realizing that I said the thought aloud. I'm aching to pull out a couple of hairs by my temple, where there's an inch and a half of fresh growth. I've been resisting the spot for months. "Harris is my brother."

A bell rings somewhere. If only this were ancient times and the ringing signified my death.

"That must be Midge," Ivy says.

I venture to touch the area by my temple; it's on the opposite side from where Ivy's sitting.

"I think we're supposed to be meeting in the theater," she says.

I poke my fingers beneath the wig, able to get a solid grip on a few strands in the time that it takes her to blink. I give them a light tug—not too strong, just enough to feel a tiny jolt. "Go ahead," I say, nodding toward the door. "The others will be waiting."

"What are you thinking?" she asks, placing a hand on my back.

I stop. My heart hammers. I release the grip on my hair, unsure if I've been caught.

"You think I'm just going to leave you here?" She grins. "No way. I'm not going anywhere without you." Her words make me tear up again. I'm not used to showing emotion in front of anyone, and the fact that I am—and that she genuinely seems to give a shit—only makes the tears flow more.

FRANKIE

SHAYLA IS SUCH A TEASE, BUT SHE'S ALSO REALLY cute, so it's hard to get her out of my head. I chase her into a theater room with Garth close at our heels.

The room is huge. A large screen hangs down, covering one wall, and there are four rows of movie seats, complete with cup holders and chairs that tilt back. I sit down in one of the seats. Shayla sits down too. But she picks the front row, away from me. And Garth parks his ass down beside her.

I can't tell if he's into her too. Or who she might be digging. She seems to be in love with just about everyone and everything, which in one way is totally annoying. But in another way it's kind of cool. I mean, it beats being around a bunch of oil-skinned cynics who think they got a raw deal in life.

Midge comes into the room. "Everyone take a seat. I've got a special surprise." She jingles her bell, commanding our attention.

But then Ivy busts in, snagging it away. "I found Taylor's cell phone," she says, holding it up.

Natalie and Parker file in behind her.

"Wait, she doesn't have her phone with her?" Shayla asks.

"Taylor used a pay phone to call me," Midge says. "Now . . . can we get back to business?"

Surprisingly—because she seems completely neurotic—Ivy backs right down. While she, Parker, and Natalie take seats in the back row, I move to the seat beside Shayla, hoping she's glad that I did (and hoping even more that Garth can take the hint). Shayla smiles at me, and I don't know what it is—how cute she is or her constant cheery disposition—but I can't help smiling back, even though I know I should be playing it cool.

"So, let's get started," Midge says, a syrupy-sweet smile on her round, puffy face. "You may have noticed some sticky-wicky things happening here at the Dark House. I don't want to give too much away—that'd be like finding out what's wrapped beneath the Christmas tree before it's time to open the gifts. But, mark my words, there's more to come."

"Meaning that we can sit back, relax, and enjoy the show, so to speak?" Parker asks.

"Enjoy it all!" She extends her arms outward like she's one of the models on a game show, presenting a brand new car. "Welcome to the Dark House, where you've come to stay, and we hope you'll play!" She bares her teeth like a rabid dog. Her eyes look freakishly wild, like they might even be dilated—like she's about to hack off all our fingers.

Midge points at the movie screen behind her, the lights go out, and music begins to play. It sounds like an old-fashioned merry-go-round—that sort of orchestral tune that's supposed to sound happy, only it's creepy and warped, and the beat's forever changing, one second too fast, the next second way too slow.

The movie screen lights up. The merry-go-round music stops, and the room goes morgue silent. Shayla grabs my arm in anticipation.

"What's happening?" I hear Ivy whisper.

The number ten appears on the movie screen, accompanied by a loud, piercing blare that hurts my ears. The noise is followed by a male voice—one that sounds old-fashioned too, like the voice-over from an old black-and-white TV commercial: "This is a test of the emergency Dark House system," the voice says. "The coordinators of your stay here, in voluntary cooperation with the Nightmare Elf, have developed this system . . . *to scare you out of your mind.* But this is not an emergency. It is a test. And if you are to survive, you need to pass it. To pass it. *To pass it, to pass it, topassittopassittopassit.*"

The words repeat over and over, faster and faster. On the screen, the number ten starts flashing. It looks three-dimensional. It's almost too bright to look at, and my eyes start to water. The ten switches to a nine. Then an eight. And then the numbers count all the way down to one.

The voice stops. It's replaced by music. I recognize the tune from my dad's collection. I can't help but sing the first line in my head: *"One is the loneliest number that you'll ever do."* I haven't heard the song in years—since my dad stopped allowing tunes in the garage, saying they were a distraction, the cause of all our screwups. Listening to Harry Nilsson belt out the lyrics reminds me of how eerie the song is. The melody is haunting. This whole scene is fantastically creepy.

Garth is giggling like a schoolgirl. I peer behind me to look at the others. Ivy's digging her fingernails into the headrest in front of her. Parker's got his hand on her back. And Natalie's sitting on the edge of her seat, winding a strand of her straw-like hair around her finger.

The number one flashes on the screen. I close my eyes, but still I can see it inside my head, pressed against my optic nerves.

Shayla's grip on my forearm tightens. "Someone make it stop," she whispers.

I find her hand in the darkness and weave my fingers through hers. Part of me wants—just for her sake—for this whole head-trippy thing to stop. But another part wants it to keep on going, so I don't ever have to let go.

I clench my teeth, anticipating a crash. It comes in the form of a scream—a heart-ripping wail that sends chills straight down my spine.

The scream is followed by a heavy thud at the back of the room, like someone or something fell.

Shayla stands from her seat, letting go of my hand. The music shuts off. The lights come on. It takes a couple of seconds for my eyes to adjust—for the orbs and color splotches to fade away. Once they do, I look around, making sure that everyone's okay and accounted for.

Everyone is. Except for Midge. She's nowhere in sight.

In her place, seated on a chair at the front of the room, is a Midge doll: round face, happy smile, fluffy white hair held back with ribbons, and a maid's uniform with tiny fake fingers sticking out from the pockets.

Garth jumps out of his seat to grab it.

"Was that Midge who screamed?" I ask.

"I think so," Ivy says. Her face is as pale as my white Irish ass. "I mean, it sort of sounded like her."

"I really hope so," Natalie mutters. But she isn't talking to us. She remains seated, staring down into her lap, having a full-on conversation by herself.

"Lookie, lookie," Garth sings, showing off his find: a cord attached to the back of the doll. He pulls it and Midge's all-too-familiar voice chirps out: *"Cakes, cookies, and pies supreme, eat up well and get ready to dream. The Nightmare Elf would like to see what we fear and then make it be."*

"Make it be?" Ivy asks.

"That doesn't make sense," Natalie pipes up, apparently done talking to herself. "We've already submitted our worst nightmares, so why would we need to re-dream them?"

"It's not exactly Steinbeck, Scarecrow," Garth says, wrapping the cord around the doll's neck. "I wouldn't take it literally." He punts the doll. The head slams against the far wall. Fake fingers go flying. The guy has absolutely no respect.

"Don't you think we should go look for Midge?" Ivy asks.

"Not before dessert," Garth says. "A little finger-collecting bird told me that it involves maggots and a bloody fountain."

"Happy yum-ness." Shayla hooks her arm with his, totally leaving me hanging.

SHAYLA

IVY'S INCESSANT NAGGING MEANS WE END UP PASSING on the dessert table to do a superficial search for Midge. We call out her name, head off in various directions, and check out all the rooms.

In the kitchen, I open the pantry closet and pull a chain that turns on an overhead light.

Holy creep-fest.

Facing me is a man's head, on a platter, with an apple wedged into its mouth. It looks completely real: gray skin, bloodshot eyes, five o'clock shadow, and bluish lips. A trickle of something orange drools out of its mouth, pooling under its chin. *Ew. Icky. Blech.* I move closer to get a better look, just as the door slams behind me. The overhead bulb goes out, replaced by two beams of bright red light, coming from the eyes of the head.

I turn back to the door. The light beams shine over the words *It's too late to turn back now*, scribbled in crayon.

I go for the knob, but it's locked. I jiggle it back and forth, telling myself not to panic—that this is obviously just a joke. "Let me out!" I shout, pounding on the door.

I search the walls—what's visible in the red light—looking for a key or some trigger that might open the door.

A heart-patterned oven mitt is there. It hangs on a hook, reminding me of Dara. I slam my back against the wall, able to picture her hanging from the ceiling.

Her body wavers. Her eyes snap open. She glares at me, pointing her dark blue finger. "There's no way out," she says.

I shake my head. Beads of sweat form at my brow.

"You weren't there for me," Dara whispers. "And so now you'll pay."

I close my eyes, then look away, but still her image is there. Her bluish face, her chalky lips, the telephone wire around her neck, and those heart-patterned socks.

I pound on the door again. I kick it, smack it, throw my weight against it.

Finally it opens.

Frankie's there, holding a bouquet of plastic machetes. "Holy shit," he says at the sight of me. He drops the machetes and I crumble into his arms.

"I'm so sorry," he says, stroking my back. "I saw you go in there and thought it'd be funny." He smells like a gas station.

Still, I press my nose against his shoulder and suck up all my tears. "I guess you got your payback."

"We'll call it even, okay?" He takes a step back to check my face. "Any chance dessert will make it better? We're done looking for Midge—for now anyway. All we're finding are props." He picks up one of the machetes and pretends to jab it in his eye. "Let's go have some lemon-filled eyeballs and intestine-layer cake."

"Sounds good," I say, taking one last peek into the closet. The heart-patterned oven mitt dangles in the red light.

In the dining room we find a platter of brains, a tray of mucous macaroons, two dozen maggot-infested cupcakes, and a plate of creamy fingers. Everything's spread out over the table, surrounding a blood-chocolate fondue fountain.

"Seriously, how did they do that?" Frankie asks, focused on the fountain.

"With red and blue food coloring mixed in," Garth says,

dipping a strawberry into the red stream. "I must say, however, this particular mixture is pretty impressive—a sophisticated consistency, made possible only with just the right amount of corn syrup." He takes a bite of his strawberry, letting the bloodred chocolate saturate his teeth.

"Gross." Ivy squeals.

"What's happenin', hot stuff?" Garth says, trying to sound like Long Duk Dong from *Sixteen Candles*, one of the greatest films ever. He waggles his tongue, exposing a barbell pierced through the center.

I let out a laugh—so loud that a weird hiccupping sound shoots out of my mouth. Garth laughs at it—at me. And we both end up doubled over as the others look on with blank faces, which just makes me laugh more.

"If Midge is supposedly missing," Frankie says, popping a lemon eyeball, "then where did all of these desserts come from? Who set up the table while she was busy disappearing?"

"Maybe she had time to set it up *before* she disappeared," Parker says. "It's all part of the plan, I'm sure."

"What plan?" Ivy asks.

"A plan in which, one by one, we all start to go missing." Garth rubs his palms together and lets out a maniacal laugh.

Meanwhile, Natalie starts muttering to herself again. She

obviously has *way* bigger problems than just a humdrum case of homesickness.

"Does your imaginary friend want some brain cake?" Garth asks her.

I stifle a giggle by feeding a chocolate worm into my mouth, happy that Garth's here. He's in this purely for the fun factor, which helps distract me from thoughts about Dara. "So, what was your nightmare?" I ask him.

He ladles some chocolate syrup into a bowl; it looks like blood soup. "I wrote about the nightmares I had when I was seven—after my dad had dared me to watch *Nightmare Elf*. I didn't want to, but he teased me into it."

"Weren't you scared to watch it?" Ivy asks.

"Sure, but with a name like Garth Vader, there really isn't much of a choice in life. You either learn to like all things scary or you end up miserable. If you're smart, you pick the first one."

"And your mom was okay with you watching it?" Ivy continues.

"My mom's at work most of the time. My dad's on disability for a bad back."

"Is she into horror too?" Parker asks.

"Negative, just like her B-type blood," Garth says. "If my mom had it her way, my dad would've dropped dead years ago, preferably from a heart attack following one of his twisted tricks."

"What kind of tricks?" I ask.

"Stupid stuff," he says, dodging the question like darts. "Anyway, my nightmare was of the typical horror-movie variety . . . getting lost in the woods, finding the Dark House, being chased down a long alleyway with villainous ghouls stalking after me."

"No big deal, then," Parker smirks.

"No big deal *anymore*," Garth says to clarify.

I study his face, wondering if his story is entirely true, or if there might be something more vulnerable beneath his seemingly resilient exterior—all his layers of dark, dark gray. "Well, if you ever want to talk about it more . . ." I say, suddenly eager to learn from him—to know how something that had caused him nightmares could wind up being something that he could fully embrace.

"*Talk?*" he asks, confusion on his face.

I nod, thinking about Dara. She'd wanted to talk too. If only I'd been more willing to listen.

GARTH

SHAYLA'S OFFER TO TALK TOTALLY TAKES ME OFF guard and I don't know what to say. What I *do* know is that I don't want her to see me like that—like someone who *needs to talk* and gets bothered by crap, and has to work out all his feelings.

Just because horror was initially forced on me doesn't mean that I didn't learn to love it, or that I need my head shrunk, or that people should feel sorry for me.

So, maybe my dad's a little messed up. Maybe he shouldn't have shown those movies to a seven-year-old, or made life for my brothers and me like a real-life horror: locking us in the basement for fun, putting red food dye in our milk, leaving us home alone so that he could prey on us like an intruder, waking us in the middle of the night made-up like a zombie or demon.

Embracing horror was a means of survival, and so far it's served me well.

After one more dip in the chocolate fountain, I suggest we head outside to continue our search for Midge. There are seven flashlights lined up on a shelf by the door. Clearly, Midge wants us to go outside. She also wants to remind us of Taylor's absence.

I open the door. It's perfectly black outside. Aside from a spotlight positioned over the door, the area is shrouded by trees; they even block out the moon. I click on my flashlight and lead the way, remembering that Tommy Tucker's nightmare chamber was several yards into the woods, but still visible through the trees. I walk away from the house, aiming the beam into the trees, trying to find a path that might lead to the chamber.

"Midge!" I call out into the night, feeling the rush of my adrenaline.

"Are you looking for the shed?" Parker asks. "And, if so, wasn't it on the other side of the house?"

"I know what I'm doing." A slight exaggeration.

"Are you sure about that?" Parker asks. "Or is the Force not quite with you?"

I let the joke slide off my back, too busy trying to eavesdrop on Shayla and Frankie. They're talking just behind me—something about Frankie's boy band back home. I can't tell if she likes him or if she's simply one of those girls who likes everyone and no one at the same time—who makes people think they actually mean something to her.

Finally I find a dirt pathway that leads into the forest. "Bingo," I say, pointing my flashlight far up the path, into the woods. But still I don't see the shed.

A few yards down the path, a rustling in the brush to the side of us sends a wave of screeches through the group. I aim my flashlight in that direction, but the rustling travels to the other side, producing more noises.

Whoosh.

Creak.

Snap.

I stop short to listen, but all I can hear is the sound of Frankie cracking up behind me. I turn to look at him just as he throws a rock into the brush, creating the source of the sounds. This guy is a total comedian.

"Midge," I sing. *"Come out, come out, wherever you are!"*

Ivy lets out a shriek. I pause and turn back again, but it's just more of her paranoia. Close behind her, Natalie's busy talking to herself, but she's smiling all the while, so apparently it's a good conversation. I wouldn't be surprised if this whole psycho-babbling bit of hers isn't fake—if she isn't trying to act like a Justin Blake–inspired character in hopes of landing herself a starring role in one of his future projects.

The back side of the shed comes into view. I turn to the others, angling my flashlight under my chin to light my face as I speak. "Are you prepared to enter Tommy Tucker's nightmare chamber?" I ask, using a throaty voice.

"Let me in, let me in!" Shayla cheers.

"Not by the hair of my chinny chin chin." I move around to the front of the shed, amazed at how authentic it looks—all boarded up and with a busted padlock on the handle, just like the real thing.

"Midge?" I call. "Are you in there?" I open the door and aim my flashlight inside as Ivy lets out a gasp.

There's a rocking chair set in the middle of the space. Seated on it, with its gloved hands neatly folded, is the Nightmare Elf doll. Between its legs is a single candle, positioned on a holder. Its flame flickers against the walls, casting a light on all of little Tommy Tucker's etchings.

"Holy shit," Frankie says.

My sentiments exactly.

With a permanent smile and bright golden hair, the Nightmare Elf is dressed in a tattered red suit, a Santa-like hat, and boots that curl up at the toe—exactly like the one in the movie. It's missing one eye from when Tommy plucked it out using a fork, just as Carson ordered.

"It has a lazy eyelid," Frankie says, squatting down for a better look. "Just like the real deal."

I nod, picturing little Tommy Tucker dragging the elf through the dirt, tying a leash around its neck, and throwing it up in the air.

Beneath the chair is a shiny black music box, just like the one that Tommy had brought along on his camping trip, the one he used to store his treasures. I open it up, shining my flashlight on Tommy's Silly Putty egg, remembering how he used the putty to make bubbles that snap.

"Will you play with me?" a high-pitched voice squeaks, nearly knocking me on my ass. I take a step back.

Ivy lets out another shriek.

It takes me a second before I realize that the voice was Frankie's. He's almost teary eyed from laughing so hard.

"Asshole," I say, though I now have a newfound respect for the guy.

I turn the crank on the music box and a familiar melody begins to play.

"'I'm a Little Teapot,'" Shayla says.

But the words are different. A little kid's voice sings them: *"I'm the Nightmare Elf, oh yes siree. Here's my hefty sack, ho, ha, hee hee. Fall asleep tonight and you will see. I'll take your nightmares and make them be."*

"Look," Shayla says, holding out her arm. She angles her flashlight over the goose bumps on her skin.

Frankie does the same, comparing the size of his goose bumps to hers.

"Let's play it again," Natalie says, taking the box from me.

I turn to check out the etchings. Words line the walls—*Die!, Torture!, Pain!*—as do sketches of ghouls, giant rats, and people with missing eyes and serpent tongues. "T. T.," I say, pointing out little Tommy Tucker's initials. Below his initials is a picture of a wolf. I run my fingers over the image, imagining that it's real, that Tommy once existed, and that this doll truly belonged to him.

There's a picture of the Nightmare Elf holding his sack of nightmares. A hand reaches out from the bulge in the sack, as though someone's trapped inside it, desperate to get out. The words above it read: *There's no escape.*

"So cool," I say, completely inspired.

"Except it isn't true." Parker's reading over my shoulder. "You escape your nightmares when you wake up."

"Sometimes," Ivy tells him. "And sometimes they haunt you

even when you're awake."

"Care to share?" I ask, curious to know what she wrote about in her contest submission.

"Check this out," Parker says, nodding to the wall by the door.

Be careful what you dream is etched into the wood. Below it is a collage of our names and seven pictures: a snake, an ax, a bear, a tombstone, a broken mirror, a noose, and a pair of demon eyes.

"Anybody want to claim their pain?" I ask.

"The gravestone," Frankie says, pointing out the image at the very bottom. "That's obviously for my nightmare."

"These images are obviously from all of our nightmares," Ivy says.

"Which one is yours?" I ask her.

Ivy looks away, toward the door. She's obviously a tease too.

Parker points to the snake. "This one's mine," he says, coming to Ivy's rescue.

"The broken mirror is mine," Natalie says.

"Mine's the noose," Shayla mutters, turning away from it.

"And mine is the ax," I tell them. "Leaving only the bear and the eyes. One must be Taylor's, and the other must be . . ." I glance at Ivy, but she refuses to look at me. "I'll bet my right nut your dream involves devil eyes. Am I right?"

"Leave her alone," Parker says.

"According to the mastermind, there's no escaping your

nightmare," I continue, talking toward the top of Ivy's head. "No escaping those eyes." I inhale the musty air, reminiscent of the basement back home, wondering how the theme of no escape will play out this weekend.

I can hardly wait to see.

Ivy

"I FREAKED AGAIN."

Back in my room, I sit on my bed, nursing a fresh cup of chamomile tea with an extra shot of lemon balm. Parker sits beside me.

"And just so you know," I continue, "I'll probably freak at least a hundred more times on this trip. But I'm hoping that each instance of freakishness will feel progressively less intense."

"Do you mind if we rewind a bit?" he asks. "You never told me why you entered the contest," he says. "Since you're not a Blake fan, I mean."

I bite my lip and gaze into his face. A lock of hair has fallen over his eye. I'd give anything to touch it.

"Trick question?" he asks.

Part of me wants to tell him the truth about my past. But I'm also afraid of what he'll think after I do. What will he think of someone who fears everyday that her parents' killer is going to come back for her?

"I thought it might look good on my college application," I lie.

"And where *are* you going to college?"

"Le Cordon Bleu. It's a culinary school in Paris."

"And the people at Le Cordon Bleu really give a crap about winning a contest to go see a horror flick?"

I feel my face turn red.

"Makes complete sense." He nods when I don't say anything. "I mean, I can totally see how that would rank right up there with participating in the French club or feeding the hungry at a soup kitchen. Now that I think about it, I seem to remember a special 'Contests Entered' section on my college applications—only with all the turkey-coloring contests I entered as a kid, and the Fourth of July toasted marshmallow–eating contests, I couldn't fit them all."

"Okay." I smirk. "You got me."

"Have I?" He bumps his shoulder against mine. The gesture sends a wave of tea over the rim of my mug, spilling into my lap.

"Crap, I'm so sorry." He gets up to fetch a rag, just as Shayla taps on the door and comes in.

"More fat and sugar?" she asks, holding a plateful of desserts from downstairs.

Parker looks back at me, straight-faced, as if less than jazzed about Shayla's impromptu visit.

"Does Natalie want to join us?" I ask, both relieved and disappointed that she's interrupted my moment with Parker.

"Natalie's holed up in our bathroom right now," Shayla says.

"Because she isn't feeling well?" I ask.

"Who knows." Shayla inserts herself between Parker and me on the bed—the Fluffernutter to our two pieces of bread. "I tried to bribe her with treats, but she says she wants to be alone. She even took her pillow and a blanket in there."

I'm pretty sure that Natalie pulls out her own hair. I almost caught her doing it earlier, but then she moved her hand away before I could fully see. I was never into hair pulling, but after the incident with my parents I started pinching—the skin on my kneecap, mostly, until it was purple, and black, and blue, and yellow.

A rainbow of dysfunction.

My way of trying to cope.

According to Dr. Donna, pinching was my way of transferring my pain and anxiety. If that theory holds true, the method never worked. Because as hard as I may've tried to transfer my pain, I always ended up with more colors, rather than less stress.

"I can go talk to her." I get up and head down the hallway to Shayla and Natalie's room. The door is open and I walk inside, past Natalie's bed. There's stationery sprawled out over her coverlet—envelopes, cards, and letterhead. There's also a fancy feather pen.

"Natalie," I call, knocking on the closed bathroom door.

"I'm fine in here." Her voice sounds all nasal-like; I'm guessing that she's been crying.

"Will you come out . . . even for a little bit? We're all just hanging out in my room, feasting on spider brownies and brain cake."

There's a loud thud against the door. It sounds like she might've kicked it. I picture her big black boots. I peer over my shoulder at the stationery, wondering what it's all about, especially since we're only here for the weekend.

I turn away and move over to her bed. Lying on the pillow is an envelope marked with her brother Harris's name. I pick it up and look back at the bathroom door, still closed.

The envelope hasn't yet been sealed.

I open it up, trying to be quiet, my eyes darting to the bathroom door. Thankfully, it remains closed. Finally, I get the envelope open and take out the card. It's a note to Harris from Natalie.

Dear Harris,

I know you're angry at me. Ever since I won this contest, something that was supposed to make me happy, it's been nothing but misery—misery for you, for Mom, for Dad. And so it's also been miserable for me.

I know you didn't want me to come here. You made that clear from the start. But it's too late to change things now. If I could I would, because nothing is worth anything if I don't have you in my corner.

I keep trying to talk to you. I'm not sure if you're listening. But I don't think I can make it through this weekend without your voice.

Love,

Natalie

I return the letter to the envelope. She must've tried calling home again. Her brother obviously doesn't want to talk to her. Still, I go downstairs to use the phone, hoping that she was the one who made the last call.

I pass the dining area—still a mess from dessert—and move into the living room. The lights are off. I flick them on, noticing a sudden chill in the air. The window over the sofa is open. The sheers blow in the breeze.

I go over to shut and lock the window, suddenly feeling like I'm being watched. I peer over my shoulder. "Natalie?" I call, wondering if she might be lurking.

No one answers. The stairway looks empty.

I glance over at the kitchen—also empty. And then I look toward the main door, assuming that it's locked. I check anyway, wrapping my hand around the knob. It turns and my heart sinks.

What if someone broke in?

I lock the door and turn to face the room again. "Midge," I attempt to call out, but my voice is far too soft.

I take a few more steps, before coming to a sudden halt, feeling my whole body tense.

Someone's there. In the closet. The door is partially open.

I can see eyes through the door crack, watching me, locked on mine.

My chest instantly tightens. I hurry into the kitchen and grab a knife from the chopping block. I begin moving toward the closet. My fingers trembling, I hold the knife down by my side. My heart hammers. I can feel the sweat at my brow.

I whisk the door open with a thwack.

No one's there.

The closet is empty.

There's just an umbrella and a pair of binoculars.

I let out a breath and rest my head against the wall, feeling a giant wave of relief. I move over to the desk, grab the phone, and press redial. The phone rings and rings, but then someone finally picks up.

"Hello?" I ask, when no one says anything. "Is someone there?"

"Who's this?" A woman's voice.

"Is this Natalie's mother?" I ask.

"Who's this?" she repeats.

"I'm a friend of Natalie's and she's here with me now . . . in Minnesota . . . on the trip to see one of Justin Blake's films. . . ."

The woman doesn't respond.

"Anyway," I continue, winding the coil cord around my fingers, "she feels really bad about coming here. She knows that you don't approve."

"Well, she's right. Her father and I *don't* approve."

"Okay, well she feels really bad," I say, knowing I'm repeating myself. "And I know that if she could do it again—go back in time, I mean—she'd make a different choice."

"What did you say your name was?"

"Ivy Jensen."

"And she's talked to you about things?"

"Well, I know how she feels about her decision to go on this trip . . . and how she feels about Harris."

"She told you about Harris?"

"Actually," I say, noticing that my fingers are completely entangled in the cord now, "I think she'd like to speak to him. Did they have a fight?"

"You have no idea what you're talking about."

"Well, maybe their falling out is something you're unaware of, a recent argument, something about this whole contest trip perhaps . . ."

"Harris is dead."

Wait. *"What?"*

"My son was stillborn," she continues. "Natalie was his twin."

"Are you sure?" I ask, thinking how stupid the question is— not to mention how insensitive.

"I think I'd know if my own son had died. A word of advice: I'd be very careful around my daughter if I were you. Now, if you'll excuse me, I have to go."

"Careful of what?"

She doesn't answer. Instead, she hangs up.

PARKER

IVY FINALLY COMES BACK INTO THE ROOM, HER FACE just as pale as it was after finding the message in Taylor's closet.

"I take it that things didn't go so well with Project Natalie?" Shayla asks, searching through Taylor's shoe rack.

"I think that maybe we should get her some help," Ivy says.

"Help, as in calling the fire department to break down the door?" Shayla asks. "Because if that's the case, you have my vote. I'm all for getting a few more hotties in the house."

"Her brother is dead," Ivy says.

"Hold up," Shayla says, trying to squeeze her foot into a

ballet slipper. "Not the brother that she's been talking about . . . not her twin . . ."

"Harris." Ivy nods. "He died at birth." She proceeds to tell us about the letter she found in Natalie's room. "I know I shouldn't have read it, but it was just lying there, and I had so many questions. And, anyway, in the letter, Natalie was apologizing to Harris for coming on this trip."

I raise my eyebrow in suspicion. "She apologized to a dead guy?"

"Hold on," Shayla says. "How do you know that he's dead?"

"I called her parents." Ivy brings her bottle pendant up to her lips. "I pushed redial after she'd called them, hoping that her brother might pick up. But her mother answered. And when I mentioned Harris's name, she told me that he was dead."

"Why would Natalie write letters to a dead person?" Shayla asks.

"Maybe it's because she's deranged," I say, stating the obvious.

"It's not just letters," Ivy says. "She talks to him too. I'm thinking that Harris is the one she's been mumbling to."

"Okay, well, I'll second Parker's notion: the girl is totally deranged . . . and I am totally depressed." Shayla tosses the ballet slipper back at the rack. "I need to go find me some big-girl shoes."

Finally, she leaves, but now there's an awkward silence between Ivy and me. I want to pick up where we left off pre–Shayla's dessert invasion, but I also don't know how to get there. After a couple more beats of silence, I pick up my mental camera, trying to imagine this as a shot.

INT. BEDROOM—NIGHT

Ivy sits down beside me on the bed. There's a plate of desserts between us.

> ME
>
> That was really cool of you to want to help Natalie.

> IVY
>
> Believe it or not, it feels good trying to help her. Somehow she seems even more messed up than me.

> ME
>
> How so?

Ivy takes a spider brownie from the plate

and chews it down, bite after bite, making
it difficult to answer.

I eat too. But after six cream-filled finger
rolls, I get up and call cut inside my head,
frustrated that it seems Ivy no longer wants
to talk.

"Don't be angry," she says. There's a smear of chocolate in the
corner of her mouth. If this were a movie, I'd lean in close and kiss
it away. "I really like you," she continues. "And I really appreciate
how sweet you've been to me. But I don't want to ruin your time
here with my drama."

I sit back down and venture to take her hand. "You're definitely not ruining my time. Whatever the reason that you decided
to enter Blake's contest, I'm really glad that you did."

She clasps her fingers around my grip and then peeks up into
my face. "Believe it or not, I am too," she says, causing my heart
to stir.

"So, then, can I ask . . . eyes or bear?"

"Huh?" Her face scrunches.

"The wall etchings."

"Oh." She looks away. Her face falls. "How about you tell me
about your snake, first," she says.

"It was actually an eel," I say to clarify, as if the distinction even matters.

"Okay." She smiles, looking back at me. "How about you tell me about your eel."

"I'd love to tell you about my eel," I smirk. "If I had an eel, that is."

"*Excuse me?*"

"Wait . . . that came out all wrong." I can feel my face changing colors. "I made the whole thing up—my nightmare submission, I mean. It was a work of fiction, inspired by something that happened when I was a kid at summer camp. I got caught in a riptide and almost drowned."

"And you had nightmares about it?"

"Not exactly, but it makes for good contest submission material, don't you think? Especially when you add in the getting-attacked-by-man-eating-eels part."

"So, you *lied*?"

"I embellished . . . and tweaked . . . and altered the facts. I'm a storyteller," I explain. "It's my job to alter the facts."

"I'll remember that," Ivy says.

"Well then, remember this: I never embellish, tweak, or alter the facts when it comes to the people I care about."

Ivy looks downward—at our hands, still clasped together—and a tiny smile forms on her face.

I look at the clock. It's almost eleven. "Hey . . ." I begin, hating the idea of leaving her alone. But before I can finish my thought, a scream comes from down the hall, slicing our moment in two.

I go for the door and peer down the hall.

Shayla is there, dressed up like Eureka Dash from the Nightmare Elf movies. "He stabbed me," she says, stumbling forward, holding her gut.

Garth comes from around the corner, dressed like Sidney Scarcella from *Hotel 9* in a suit jacket with tails and a blood-stained apron. There's a demented smile on his face.

Shayla tries to grab the wall for support, but ends up collapsing to the floor.

"Holy shit!" I shout, rushing into the hallway. I scoot down to assess her wound, pulling up on the hem of her blouse.

"Not so fast!" she hollers, slapping my hand away. "You have to at least buy me dinner first."

Both she and Garth start laughing.

"Die, you lowly peasant," Garth says, pretending to stab his plastic knife into her back.

Shayla sits up and runs a finger over her blood-chocolate-smeared stomach. "You guys totally have to check out the costume closet downstairs," she says, licking said finger.

Frankie peeks out into the hall, a guitar strapped across his chest. "Can you guys keep it down?"

"Good night," I say, returning to the room and shutting the door. Shutting Ivy and me off from the rest of them—for a little while at least.

We end up lying in bed—me on Taylor's and Ivy on her own—facing one another, with the lights kept dim. We spend the next couple hours talking about everything—about favorite ice cream and famous couples. And best movie kisses (for her, that scene in *Breakfast at Tiffany's*, when Holly and Paul share a kiss in the rain while "Moon River" plays in the background; for me, the upside-down kiss between Spider-Man and Mary Jane).

"Do you have a boyfriend?" I ask, surprised to hear the words come out my mouth.

"No." She bites back a smile. Her cheeks turn pink.

I wait for her to reciprocate the question, but she doesn't. "I should probably let you get some sleep," I say, feeling a major blow to my ego.

"Don't go," she says. Her eyes widen. "Let's talk some more."

"About what?" I ask, hoping she'll finally open up about her nightmares, but she asks me about favorite comic book characters instead.

Finally, around three a.m., after we've explored just about every topic, except the one she refuses to discuss—the one involving her contest submission—we decide to call it a night.

She slips beneath the covers and closes her eyes. I close my eyes too. But there's no way I'm going to fall asleep. I toss and turn, flip and flop, finally resolving to wait it out until morning and watch her sleep.

I could seriously watch her all night, admiring her inky-black lashes against her pale ivory skin, the curves of her body beneath the coverlet, and those raspberry-colored lips.

But then her eyes snap open and I'm totally caught.

"I can't sleep," she says.

"Me neither."

"Are you feeling anxious too?"

"More like restless," I tell her. "What are you feeling anxious about?"

"Would you mind holding me for a little while?" she asks, in lieu of an answer. "At least until I fall asleep."

My heart absolutely pounding, I move to her bed and lay down on top of the covers while she remains beneath them. She rolls over and I hold her, savoring the warmth of her back against my chest. She smells like chamomile and chocolate—like something I want to bottle up and wash all over me.

In the movie version of my life, I'd have met her someplace

else—while vacationing somewhere tropical, maybe. We'd fall in love with both the island and each other, unable to part at the end of our stay. My favorite scene would be the one where the camera zoomed in as we kissed—in the ocean, while it rained—with the balmy beach air crushing against our skin like velvet. A kiss that would top both Spidey's and Holly's any day.

NATALIE

IVY WENT THROUGH MY STUFF. I KNOW SHE DID.

I almost opened the door. My hand was wrapped around the knob. My mind was flashing forward to what would happen if I confronted her.

But I didn't, because it feels safer in here—more controlled, less influenced by time.

How long have I been away from home?

How long has it been since Harris spoke to me?

How long ago did I call my parents?

Sitting with my back against the tub, I look down at the

strands of hair collected on the bath mat, between my knees. Twenty-six.

One-hundred-eighty-two wall tiles. Forty-three floor tiles. Thirty-six tissues in the box. Ninety-two squares of toilet paper. Three bars of soap. Five travel bottles of shampoo. Two drinking cups.

Someone screams. The sound echoes the screaming deep inside me. I grab the hair strands and get up, unlock the door, and take a step outside. Shayla's out in the hallway. She's dressed like Eureka from *Nightmare Elf*. Garth is with her, dressed as Sidney Scarcella. They're both laughing.

I close the door, move over to the sink, and toss the hair strands into the basin. Ever since I left home, I've been itching for another tattoo: Harris's beating heart, right over my own. When I was ten and wrote his name 311 times on my body, and my dad told me that I wasn't worthy of having Harris's name inked on my skin, I believed him. I *wasn't* worthy.

But maybe Harris would think otherwise. Maybe it would even get him to start talking to me again.

I take off my T-shirt and remove the towels I've placed over the mirror, squinting my eyes to avoid the whole picture. I pluck a lipstick from my pocket and draw the heart right over my own.

It doesn't come out right the first time—too pointy at the bottom, too narrow at the top. I wipe the mark and try again on the other side of my chest. But it looks more like a potato. I wipe once more and give it another shot. At least ten attempts later, my chest is covered in lipstick smudges and smears, and so are my palms. And the side of my face.

A floorboard creaks. Someone's here. Outside the door. There's another knock. "Natalie?" Shayla's voice. "I have to get in there. I made a bloody mess of myself—literally—and I need to wash up."

I ignore her and rip off my wig. My heart pounds at the image. I hate the way I look. I probably even hate it more than my parents do. My real hair, beneath the wig, is the same dark color. I dyed it. And pulled out big chunks—what started out as single strands. Now, it's long in some places and short in others, with a gaping bald spot in the back and a few smaller ones on both sides. Too noticeable without the wig. Too much to cover up.

"*Hello?*" she shouts, knocking again. Luckily there's a lock. "We called your parents, by the way," she adds. "We asked them about Harris. Can you guess what they might've said?"

Sure, I can guess. Did they say that I was crazy? That I talk to myself? That I'm a constant disappointment? Did they mention that I preoccupy myself with things they don't understand? That when Harris died eighteen years ago, the expectations for me were doubled? But who could possibly live up to the achievements of two people, particularly when one of those people is a baby who probably sacrificed himself for his twin before he was even born? But still, I've tried. I study hard. I get good grades. I volunteer at church. But that's nowhere near enough. And I don't know what else to do—I don't know what else I *can* do.

Shayla knocks again. "Come out here and I'll tell you what they said."

I run the faucet, hoping she'll go away. I pick at my lips—the dry skin—rolling it between my fingertips.

"I'll give you ten seconds," Shayla says, talking to me like I'm three. She counts aloud, pausing between each number.

Until she gets to ten.

I take a deep breath and grab a three-strander from behind my ear. I yank, feeling a wave of relief swim through my veins. I check out the strands. I got the follicles, too.

"She's going to come in," a voice whispers.

"Harris?" At last. My whole body tingles.

The bathroom door whips open.

Shayla is there.

She stares at my reflection in the mirror—my patchy scalp, my bloodshot eyes, and the red-lipstick smudges on my face, neck, and chest. Her lips peel open in revulsion and then retract back in what looks like remorse; they purse tight, her brow furrows. Her expressions aren't so much unlike my parents' when they walked in on me in the bathroom back home and saw my very first tattoos. Only, unlike Shayla, my parents' remorse had nothing to do with invading my privacy, and everything to do with my very existence. At least that's what I believe. At least that's how they make me feel.

FRANKIE

AFTER A MOSTLY SLEEPLESS NIGHT—BECAUSE I WAS anxious about meeting Justin Blake—I didn't end up nodding off until sometime around five a.m.

It's now after one and I'm just getting out of bed. I grab a shower, and step out of the tub, startled to find the words THERE'S NO ESCAPE written on the mirror, through the steamed glass.

I look around, making sure that I'm alone. And then I move closer to touch one of the letters, able to feel a thick coating of wax.

I'm seriously going to miss this place.

Once dressed, I head downstairs to look for Shayla,

disappointed that she didn't come into my room last night while I was playing guitar, practicing the song I wrote for Justin Blake, inspired by *Nightmare Elf*. I brought along the sheet music, hoping to give it to Blake as a gift, but it'd be even more amazing if he'd let me play the song for him on the Slipknot Telecaster.

"Good afternoon," Ivy says, standing at the kitchen island. She's made some egg thing—a big casserole dish of it. There are also pans full of bacon and potatoes. "Midge still remains among the missing," she says. "I say *among* because Taylor's still missing too. But I thought I'd make some food anyway." She grabs a cantaloupe half and begins slicing it up with the precision of an Iron Chef—fast and furious, making perfectly symmetrical slices. She does the same with the other half, the blade so close to her fingers that I feel myself squirm.

"Yikes," I say, when she's finally done.

Parker's watching too. "Remind me not to get on your bad side."

I take a step closer to grab a slice, and that's when I see her. Shayla.

She stares at me from the living room sofa. My first reaction is excitement. But then I notice that the sofa's been pulled out to a bed, and that there are blankets strewn about. Garth sits up from a heap of them. They obviously spent the night together.

"Hey," she says, smiling at me, like it's no big deal—like she hasn't been openly flirting with me since the moment I climbed into that hearse.

"Hungry?" Parker asks them.

"Starving." Garth stands from the sofa and stretches his arms wide.

"Can somebody go get Natalie?" Ivy asks. "Everything's just about done."

"I'll go," I say, desperate for a moment to myself. I round the corner and let out a breath, trying to pull the invisible dagger out of my heart, but it's wedged in way too deep. I guess I'm not so used to letting myself get hurt.

After a few seconds, I climb the stairs. The door to Natalie's room is partially open. She's sitting on her bed, gazing down at her suitcase.

"Hey," I say, edging the door open wider.

"Did they tell you?" she asks.

"Did *who* tell me *what*?"

"The others . . . about me."

"Apparently not, because I have no idea what you're talking about."

"Neither do they."

"Translation?" This chick is so messed up.

"Was that you playing the guitar last night?" she asks, switching gears. "Because if so, you're really talented."

"Thanks. Do you play?"

"No, but my brother does. I really wish that he were here. He and I don't usually go more than an hour without talking." She keeps her focus toward her heavy black boots.

I glance down at my infinity bracelet, suddenly feeling sorry for her. "I know what it's like to miss someone."

"Are you talking about your mom or your uncle?"

"My mom," I say, impressed that she was so tuned in at the dinner table.

"Why did she leave?"

"I ask myself that all the time. I guess she didn't want to be married anymore, or didn't want to be a mom anymore. I don't know. I don't know if I'll *ever* know."

"Who wouldn't want to be a mom to someone like you?"

The comment takes me off guard and I can't help but grin. "My mom and I used to have a lot of fun together. We'd go for long walks. She'd point out different types of birds, plants, flowers, trees . . . everything was an adventure with her. Sometimes I wonder if it wouldn't have been easier for me if she'd died along with my uncle. Growing up, it was way worse knowing that she was alive—that she was choosing to be away."

"So, how are you able to go on?"

"Well, you can't stop living," I tell her. "Otherwise, we might as well be dead too."

"I just don't know what I'm supposed to do," she says. "I mean, I want to meet Justin Blake and see the movie. But part of me feels like I should go home early—like I don't deserve those things since I came here without permission."

"Give yourself permission. Live your own life, make your own choices. Because going home early—punishing yourself—isn't going to change the fact that you came here to begin with."

"Is that what you do . . . give yourself permission, I mean?"

"It's easier said than done," I admit, thinking about all the times that my dad's dumped on my plans by having me work overtime, and how I haven't exactly spoken up. "But I try to have my own voice—at least most of the time."

"Your own voice," she repeats. Her eyes grow big as if what I've said is gospel.

"Now, come on." I hold out my hand, confident that whatever's bugging her is more than just a couple of days away from her brother. "Ivy's whipped up an IHOP-worthy brunch."

Surprisingly, Natalie places her hand in mine and together we go downstairs.

SHAYLA

I SPENT THE NIGHT WITH GARTH. AND IT WAS REALLY nice—until it wasn't. Until it got all awkward and I wanted to go back upstairs.

It happened like this: after the costumes, neither of us was ready to end the night. Frankie was playing a guitar right upstairs, and the music made it easy for Garth and me to sink into the comfort of the living room sofa getting to know each other better.

We spent much of the night in hysterics, which is exactly how I suspected things would be. But soon things got heated, and I found myself cuddled against his chest, playing with the tear in his T-shirt—one long rip across his navel.

I could tell that he wanted to kiss me. The truth is, I wanted to kiss him, too—to feel what it's like to kiss someone who has a hoop pierced through his lip and a barbell through his tongue.

He moved a little closer and stared straight into my eyes. "Shayla?" he asked. His lips—that silver hoop—were just inches away from mine. "Do you ever go for guys like me back home?"

The truth is that I don't, but I sure as hell wanted to try. "Guys like *you*?" I decided to play dumb.

"Yeah, you know . . . dark, slightly twisted, not exactly the most popular."

"I go for all types of guys," I say, stretching the truth like bubble gum.

"Good." He was staring at my mouth now.

I closed my eyes, anticipating the kiss. Not two seconds later, I went for it. The hoop was cold and hard against my lip and had a slightly metallic taste.

The barbell made more of an impact. It teased against my tongue, glided across the skin—kind of nice at first, but then it seemed like he was working it too hard, trying to impress me with too much rubbing, which caused a nasty buildup of saliva.

I pulled away and flashed him a smile that told him that I

liked it. "I'm really curious," I said, poking my finger through the T-shirt tear. "When you were talking before about your nightmare . . . How were you able to end up loving something that had once given you bad dreams?"

Evidently, I'd found the mood breaker, because his body language changed. He looked away. His jaw tensed. "I just did." He shrugged.

"Yes, but *how*?"

He straightened up on the sofa then, pushed me off him, and got up for more dessert. He gulped down a mouthful of chocolate and let it drool down his chin.

But this time it wasn't funny.

After that, we pretty much took opposite ends of the sofa, not really talking to each other. I was done with the fun and games, and apparently that's all he was willing to offer.

He and I are sitting at the dining room table now, pretending like there isn't a giant elephant in the room. Natalie comes to join us, with her own fleet of elephants in tow—none of which involves Frankie, though they *are* holding hands.

I busted in on her in the bathroom last night—thanks to her letter opener—and saw some of what she's been trying to keep under wraps: some sections of her hair are shoulder length, while others are barely an inch long. She's also bald in spots—places where she must've pulled the hair out; there was a wad of strands in the sink. If all that wasn't disturbing enough, she was covered in lipstick.

I told her I was sorry and offered to talk, but in that moment she couldn't really speak, and I didn't know who was more shocked—me by what I saw, or her because I was seeing it.

Ivy takes a seat at the table, having prepared a feast. It's kind of annoying how good she looks in the morning, despite having no makeup on and her hair pulled back in an old-lady bun.

"I wish I could cook like this," I tell her.

"Thanks. It's sort of my thing." She seems far more relaxed than I've seen her yet.

"*I* need a thing," I tell her. "Traveling, I guess. You should see all the maps and postcards hanging on the wall in my room upstairs. Seeing them just makes me want to go everywhere."

"I'm surprised that *you've* even seen them," Frankie says. "You haven't exactly spent too much time in your room, have you?" He raises his eyebrow at me.

"What's that supposed to mean?" I ask, knowing what he's insinuating, but I'm not really in the mood for drama. My head aches. I need more sleep. One of the sofa springs dug into my hip last night, and now the muscle's sore. I rub at my temples, relieved that Frankie doesn't say anything else.

"So," Garth says, breaking the beat of silence. He leans across the table to Natalie. "Shayla tells me that your brother's dead."

"*Seriously?*" I let my fork drop to the plate. I mean, could he have any less tact?

"Is he the person you've been mumbling to?" Garth asks her. "Of course, I have my own theories on the subject."

"You don't know anything about me," she says.

"That's true," Ivy says. "We don't. But that doesn't mean we wouldn't like to get to know you."

"What's up with the mirrors?" Garth asks.

"Catoptrophobia," Parker explains. "A fear of mirrors and/or one's reflection. It can stem from poor self-image or urban legends associated with the supernatural . . . like the magic mirror in *Snow White*, for example."

"And you know this because . . . ?" Garth asks.

"Because the lead character in the screenplay I'm working on has catoptrophobia. He was traumatized after watching his sister play Bloody Mary at a sleepover. You know, the game where you summon evil spirits to appear in the bathroom mirror."

"So, which camp are you in?" Garth asks, focused on Natalie again. "Poor body image or supernatural sufferer?"

"I just hate my reflection," she says, as if she belongs in another camp altogether.

"Is that why you cover yourself up?" I ask. "Which is completely ridiculous, by the way, because you know you'd be totally gorgeous, right?"

"Have you ever tried to talk to someone about it?" Ivy asks. "A therapist, I mean?"

"I'm the product of therapy, and you can see how well that's worked out," Garth jokes.

"Yeah. Me too," Ivy says.

"Me three." Natalie smirks. "Harris is the only one who understands me."

"Okay, but Harris is *dead*," Garth says.

"Not to me, he isn't. I don't expect any of you to get it, but he talks to me. I hear his voice inside my head."

"The voice of a dead man?" Garth grins.

"*I* believe that stuff," Ivy says. "I think there are people who can communicate with those who've passed on."

"For me, it's only Harris," Natalie says. "And he hadn't spoken to me since the moment I got on the plane to come on this trip, even though I'd been continuing to talk to him. But then, last night, in the bathroom, he whispered a little something."

"A little *what* thing?" Frankie asks. "You make him sound so real."

"He *is* real—*very* real to me."

"I wish I could communicate with the dead," I tell them. "My best friend Dara hung herself, and I have so many unanswered questions."

"What's your biggest question?" Ivy asks.

"If she knows how much I cared about her, I guess."

"Why wouldn't she?" Garth's eyebrow raises.

I shrug, feeling suddenly self-conscious. "Maybe because I wasn't exactly there for her in the way that I could've been. She was pretty much a social outcast at my school. And instead of constantly trying to defend her, sometimes I just played along. I mean, I know it wasn't right, but being with Dara became social suicide for me."

"But real suicide for her," Garth says, stabbing me with the truth.

"Why didn't people like her?" Natalie asks.

"There was no one thing." I shift uneasily in my seat. "She just wasn't into the same stuff that the rest of us were, and that kind of brought down the group."

"Stuff like what?" Ivy asks.

"You know." I shrug again. My face feels hot. "The whole social scene at school—trying to get invited to A-list parties and go to A-list clubs. Dara didn't care about that stuff. She'd even go out of her way to reject it. Like, if I snagged her an invite to a party, she'd arrive underdressed."

"Imagine that," Garth says, poking a finger through the hole in his T-shirt.

"But it's more than that," I say, remembering a wear-red-for-love fund-raiser party when Dara showed up in blue-jean overalls and insinuated that Amanda's family was gluttonous for owning three homes and four cars.

"It's really hard to explain, but she wasn't doing anything to help her situation," I continue, "which was really frustrating to watch. I saw her becoming more and more isolated. And I know I definitely should've done something, because I knew that behavior wasn't *her*. Dara was so much better than all of that. But I distanced myself instead."

"And so now you feel responsible?" Ivy asks.

"Not responsible." I swallow hard. "I just wish I'd have known how unhappy she was. I mean, I knew she was depressed, but I never pegged her as suicidal." I look around for a wall vent, wondering if the air conditioner is on, if anyone thinks it's as humid as I do. "Anyway, it happened a little over two years ago, and I still dream about it—about finding her body and about how alone she must've felt—but, unlike some of you, I didn't go to therapy. I discovered Justin Blake. During the weeks following Dara's funeral, there were round-the-clock marathons of his films. And, since I wasn't really sleeping much back then, his movies were the perfect distraction to my own horror."

"Cheers to that," Natalie says, raising her coffee mug. "Justin Blake's movies: the very best form of therapy."

We all raise our mugs to toast. A moment later, a cuckoo bird comes out from its birdhouse-clock to alert us to the time, only instead of just making a simple chirping sound, it starts to sing: *"Greetings, Dark House Dreamers, it's almost time for fright. The Nightmare Elf promises to visit you all tonight."*

"Holy crap," Ivy mutters, panic mode returned.

"Only one more hour to go," Garth says, rubbing his palms together.

I want to share his enthusiasm, but suddenly I want to go home.

GARTH

THE HEARSE PULLS UP AT FOUR P.M. SHARP. I couldn't be more stoked. Shayla comes and stands beside me as we pile into the back. I'd rather she kept her distance. I'm really sick of her bullshit, pretending that she's all into me, only to want to get inside my head and excavate something that isn't there.

She ends up sitting between Ivy and Parker. "So, was anybody able to dig up the details on this confidential, *Nightmare Elf*–inspired film project?" she asks.

"It seems to be totally hush-hush," Parker says. "Everything online and in the trades says that Blake's filming in Beijing."

"'Hence the confidential-project part," I tell them.

"Even this contest was on the down-low," Frankie says. "I couldn't find it on Blake's Web site, and when I went back to the fan site a week or so after I sent in my essay, the contest post was no longer there."

"Blake's peeps probably took it down, tired of reading all of the entries—over twenty thousand supposedly." I yawn. "Anyway, I'm sure Blake's chartered a private jet to fly him back to Beijing after the filming tonight."

"What are the odds that I'd be able to sneak myself onto that jet?" Shayla giggles.

"I'd say they suck pretty hard-core," I tell her.

She shoots me a dejected look, which honestly warms my heart.

We drive for more than two hours before pulling onto a gravel road, lined on both sides with trees. Parker takes out his video camera, rolls down the window, and starts filming.

"Are you lost?" Frankie shouts to the driver as we get thicker into the forest.

The hearse rocks from side to side as the terrain beneath us gets more unstable. At one point I'm not even sure if the car's width will make it through the trees. Branches scrape and poke the windows and doors.

"You know this is killing your paint job, right?" Frankie calls out to the driver.

Finally we reach a clearing, but the tree boughs overhead block out most of the light. The driver—the same guy who picked me up from the airport—puts the car in park and gets out. At first I think he must be going to check on the damage, but instead he opens the door. "It's a little too narrow to drive," he says. "But we can get there on foot. It's just on the other side of these trees."

"What is?" Parker asks.

"Harris says we shouldn't go," Natalie whispers.

"Your dead brother Harris, right?" I say, intentionally being obnoxious.

We follow the driver down the long narrow roadway. It's several minutes of walking before the entire area in front of us opens up.

It's like something straight out of a dream. WELCOME, DARK HOUSE DREAMERS is lit up in Gothic lettering, hanging above an entrance gate. There's also a Ferris wheel, a merry-go-round, and a ride called Hotel 9; with multiple pointed roofs, it looks like the hotel in the movie.

There's a tall iron gate that surrounds the entire area, keeping it from the public. It's got to be at least thirty feet tall. There's also barbed wire threaded through and around the rungs at the very top. "What the hell is this?" Parker asks.

"It was an old abandoned amusement park, from what I hear," the driver says. "But it's been revived just for you, the Dark House Dreamers."

"Okay, but I didn't sign up for an amusement park," Parker says. "I'm here to see a movie."

"Well, perhaps you should get your ticket." The driver motions to the gate. "But first . . ." He pulls what appears to be a red handkerchief from the inner pocket of his jacket, only when he opens it up and shakes it out, it's actually a red sack, just like the Nightmare Elf's. "Please deposit any cell phones, cameras, or video equipment inside here." He gives Parker a pointed look.

"You can't be serious," Parker says.

"I *am* serious." The driver smiles. "If you want to see the movie, you'll honor Mr. Blake's request to deposit your electronic belongings here." He gives the empty sack a shake.

"And if we don't make a deposit?" Parker persists.

"Then no movie and no Blake," the driver says.

Frankie checks his cell phone for a signal. "Still nothing."

"So, then, it's not like it even matters," Shayla says, checking her cell phone too. "Except I *did* want to get a photo of myself with Blake." She keeps a firm hold on her camera. "It was a birthday present last year," she explains. "Just in time for my two-week sojourn to Prague."

"Rest assured, there will be plenty of photo opportunities later," the driver says. "Now, shall we?"

I place my camera and phone down into the sack. Shayla and the others follow suit.

"Very good," the driver says, tying the bag closed. "Now, without further ado . . ." He pulls something else from his pocket—a remote control—and points it at the front gates. The doors open to the sound of music—the same whacked-out carnival tune that played back at the Dark House.

The merry-go-round begins to revolve. The Nightmare Elf's fat little face goes round and round at the top. I move closer, standing just inside the gate now. There's a roller coaster called Creeper Coaster and a giant tree house called Forest of Fright. A wooden cutout of Eureka from the Nightmare Elf movies—dressed in her peasant blouse and '70s jeans—stands in front of a snack shack, holding a tray full of fried dough and popcorn.

It's way too incredible to be real: the blinking lights, the music, and the images from his films, brought to life, like on a movie set. All of it is hidden—here—in the woods. And to think that it was just forty-eight hours ago that I was hanging out in my parents' basement, filling out applications to work at random gas stations and liquor stores.

"This place is unbelievable," I say. "I mean, if I didn't already think that Justin Blake was a creative genius, this pretty much seals the deal."

A flat-screen TV lights up a few yards in front of us. We move in closer. And that's when we hear it.

Clamp.

Bang.

Bolt.

The park gates close. The driver threads a chain through and around the bars.

"Wait, what are you doing?" Parker asks him.

"Enjoy!" the driver hollers. He gives us a soldier's salute before turning away, heading back down the dirt path.

There's static on the TV screen now; it's followed by a black background that keeps flipping.

And then I see it. On the screen. Justin Blake's face. It has a grainy quality, but it's unmistakably him.

"Hello, Dark House Dreamers," he says.

"Hello," Shayla shouts back, silently clapping her hands.

"I hope you all had a pleasant journey to picturesque Hundley County," he winks, knowing full well how lame this area is, "and that you're all enjoying the Dark House."

"Definitely," Shayla cheers.

"So, now that you've gotten a slight taste of the weekend, let's see to it that you get a full dose of what you came here for. After all"—he leans in closer to the camera, and his pale blue eyes widen for effect—"you came here to be scared, didn't you?"

"Yeah!" Frankie shouts, pumping his fist.

Natalie stands in front of us all. Her hands are clasped together and she's mumbling to herself, most likely auditioning for a future role.

"Okay," Blake says, but the word actually comes out "o-*kee-ay*." There's so much static interference going on: a crunching sound in the background and an annoying buzz. Add that to the fact that the screen continues to flip, and that there's a perpetual zigzag that cuts through his face, and it's hard to get the full *him*.

"So, let's get down to why you're *really* here, shall we?" he asks. "You want a behind-the-scenes look at my latest project, don't you?"

"Yes!" I shout, clapping my hands. I give Parker and Ivy a sideways glance. They're hanging on Blake's every word, as if we're all going to be tested later.

"You told me your worst nightmares," Blake continues. "That was your ticket into the gate. And let me just say in response to that"—he leans in closer again, his eyes bugging out like a deranged serial killer—"revealing your biggest nightmare probably wasn't the best idea."

Shayla squeals in anticipation.

It's extra grainy on the screen. Blake says a bunch more stuff, but none of us can hear him. The audio's all out of whack. ". . . to face your biggest fears," he continues, but the words aren't in sync with his lips. The speed must be off.

A moment later, the screen goes black.

"What the hell?" I shout.

It fades back a couple of seconds later, but Blake is no longer there. In his place, hidden among shadows, is someone dressed up as the Nightmare Elf; I can just make out his bright red suit and the chubby cheeks on his elf mask.

"The reason you're here is far more paramount than just a behind-the-scenes look at my film," the elf says, in a voice that isn't Blake's. "This park is the set of my new movie. And you are my stars."

"Seriously?" Shayla asks; her inflated ego just got bigger. "We're the actors?"

"The camera's already rolling," the elf says. "So, enjoy the park. Walk around, have a snack, go on all of the Justin Blake movie–themed rides as many times as you like. A word to the wise, however: the Eureka Shrieker is a real killer." He holds the sides of his head.

Ivy looks like she's about to hurl.

"But . . . but . . . but," the elf continues, "before you begin, there's something you need to know. There are rides and challenges tailored for each of you, based on your essay. If you want to make it to the final cut, you—and you alone—will have to face your nightmare by going on that ride. Anyone who enters another Dark House Dreamer's nightmare will be unable to attend the rough-cut showing at the end with the *real* creative genius."

"J.B.," Shayla whispers.

The elf's voice goes grave-serious: "Find your ride and face your fear. Any problems, including if you chicken out, just use the emergency phones. Now, what are you waiting for?" He unleashes a maniacal laugh that impresses even me. The TV screen fades to black.

"Holy freaking shit!" I shout. "I mean, do you seriously get what this means?"

"We're going to be in a movie!" Shayla bursts.

"With no script, directions, or rehearsals?" Parker asks, already trying to poke holes.

"Sort of like the reality-TV version of a major motion picture," Shayla says. "Has that even been done yet? Or are we breaking some serious new ground here?"

Tears well up in my eyes. An opportunity like this could honestly change everything for me—show everyone who ever doubted me. My dad is going to freak.

While the others point out some of the video cameras

positioned around the park, wannabe–Linda-Blair Natalie runs back to the entrance gate. She looks outward, through the bars, wiping an invisible layer of sweat from her brow.

"What's wrong?" Frankie asks her, obviously buying her bogus act.

Instead of answering, Natalie struggles to get the gate to open, pulling at the chain and shaking the lock. "Harris says we're trapped," she shouts.

"And Harris is as dead as last night's dinner," I say, still thinking about those amazing ribs.

"It's hard to be trapped when there are emergency phones," Shayla says. "Plus, I thought he stopped talking to you."

"He's started again. *Remember?*"

"Well, tell him to shut up," I say. "Because we're here to be in a movie. So let's get to it."

Natalie turns away from the gate, and we all move deeper inside the park.

IVY

I'M PROBABLY THE ONLY PERSON HERE WHO ISN'T completely enamored with Justin Blake and/or his work, and yet watching him on the overhead TV screen just now, and listening to whoever it was dressed as the Nightmare Elf say that we need to face our fears . . . it felt like they were talking directly to me.

The others seem excited to be here. Garth smiles for the camera as he poses with a wooden cutout of one of Justin Blake's characters (some girl with a big floppy hat and bell-bottom jeans). Shayla hams it up, squealing and giggling extra loud, as she plays that game where you slam a mallet as hard as you can, trying to get a puck (in this case, the Nightmare Elf) to jump up and ring the bell at the very top. She doesn't manage it on the first couple of tries, but then Frankie takes a crack at it, sending the Nightmare Elf soaring; the elf's head slams against the bell, causing the latter to ring and the elf's tongue to stick out from the impact.

Natalie, on the other hand, has the hood of her jacket up now, even though it's at least eighty degrees. She's repositioned her scarf, too, so that it covers her mouth and chin. A pair of oversize sunglasses conceals her eyes. I gaze up at a video camera, noticing that she's positioned away from it. Being videotaped must bother her—the idea of seeing herself later on film. I don't want to be videotaped either—don't want to risk that my parents' killer might one day recognize me in a movie.

"So, what do you think?" Parker asks, standing at my side.

"I'm not really sure *what* to think. I didn't ask to be in a movie."

"What's wrong? Don't want to be a reality star?"

I wish I could read his mind to know if he's thought about last night, because it's been on my mind all day. He was so incredibly sweet, staying in my room, and then holding me when my anxiety got too big.

"Hey, come check this out!" Shayla says. She's moved farther into the park, past a merry-go-round with evil-looking horses. There's another ride tucked behind it, but only the back side is visible: a yellow house with a picket fence.

I wonder if it's mine.

"It's the greenroom," Shayla shouts. "Come on!"

Movie screens light up around the park showing films by Justin Blake. I look back at the house, eager to get away from it. I follow the others to where Shayla is. It's a lounge area, set up with patio sofas and chairs. There are food coolers positioned about, as well as a couple of portable refrigerators. "Seven chairs," I say, nodding toward a dining area, reminded of Taylor's absence.

"Over here," Frankie says, calling us to one of the rides. "Check it out. This ride goes underground." He points out where a tunnel burrows down into the ground and then comes out several yards later.

The rest of the Nightmare Elf's Train of Terror looks fairly normal—like a basic roller coaster—with individual carts that resemble the Santa-like sacks that the Nightmare Elf always carries. The elf's chubby face is positioned in front of the very first cart. His eyes are aglow, the pupils flashing red.

Shayla climbs into the cart at the very front.

"Wait, how do you know you can ride this?" Parker checks out the ride's signage—basically a board that lists rules about staying properly restrained—obviously heeding the Nightmare Elf's message that, in addition to our personalized nightmare rides, we're only allowed to go on rides that are based on Justin Blake's movies.

"This ride is E for everyone," Shayla says, suddenly a park expert. She peeks up at the camera and sticks out her chest. "An equal opportunity thriller." She blows the camera a kiss.

Garth jumps into the cart behind her. "You'll probably want to sit this one out," he says to Natalie. "I don't think Harris would approve."

Instead of taking his remark with its intended sarcasm, Natalie's face falls flat. "You're right," she says. "Harris wants me to find a way out of here." She looks around at the perimeter of the park in a halfhearted search for an exit. When she doesn't immediately see one, she climbs into one of the carts, careful to keep all her layers of shrouding intact.

"Shall we?" Parker asks, motioning to the two train carts behind Frankie's.

I climb inside the first one. Parker steps into the cart behind it. He presses the start button, on a post by the list of rules. Everyone's handlebars drop down, locking us into place.

At the same moment, the Nightmare Elf lets out a childlike giggle. *"Hold on to your chair,"* the elf sings. *"Because I'm ready to scare."*

Shayla, Garth, and Frankie cheer in unison.

I clench the handlebars. A motor starts up somewhere beneath me, under my seat. The train carts begin to coast into a tunnel, before spiraling downward into a deep, dark hole.

"We're going underground!" Shayla shouts.

The Nightmare Elf lets out another laugh. *"Too late to turn back now."*

My stomach drops. I lurch forward, feeling like I'm going to fall out of my seat.

One of us howls. Someone else lets out a scream.

Finally, the carts level out and proceed in a forward direction again. But still there's only darkness. "Parker?" I call out, but I can barely hear my own voice.

The wheels rip across the tracks, screeching over any other sound.

I grip the handlebar tighter. My teeth clench harder. I close my eyes, trying to breathe through my anxiety. I'm stronger than my fears, bigger than this moment. I inhale and then exhale, blowing out my negative thoughts, trying to return to a state of calm.

The wind blows at my face, through my hair. And, for just a second, I almost convince myself that this is actually kind of fun.

But then my cart comes to a sudden halt.

And the screeching noise stops.

There's just the pumping of my heart—so hard and heavy inside my chest that I can hear it in my ears, can feel it in my veins.

The lights remain out. I can't see a thing—not the person seated in front of me, nor the hand before my face.

Is it over? Are we stuck? Why isn't anyone saying anything?

I can hear the sound of water trickling. A leaking pipe, maybe. I reach forward to touch Frankie, but there's just empty space in front of me. Our carts must've disconnected, or maybe they were never connected to begin with.

"Parker?" I call, hearing the tremor in my voice.

He doesn't answer. Instead, it's another voice that cuts through the darkness: a child's voice, whispering something, but it's far too faint to hear.

"Hello?" I call out.

I strain to hear, able to make out the words *victim* and *doomed*. Should I get out of my cart? Try to find my way out? Is it possible that my cart went off the tracks?

A light clicks on over my head, making me squint. Finally, I can see.

An image of two boys waivers a few yards away. They look freakishly real. Dressed in tuxedos, the boys have slick black hair and stark white faces. Their eyes stare in my direction.

"Hello?" I repeat, but no sound comes out. There's a sharpness inside my chest, making it hard to breathe.

Music begins to play—piano keys tap out the tune to "Three Blind Mice." *"Seven blind mice. Seven blind mice,"* the boys begin to sing. *"See how they run. See how they run. They think they can get away from me, but I have another plan, you see.*

Fall asleep in the Dark House and you will be, seven dead mice. Seven dead mice."

They smile at the same time—dark red lips, bright white teeth—and begin walking toward me.

I pull on the handlebar, but it won't budge, trapping me in place. "No!" I shout. My forehead's sweating. My mouth turns dry.

I shimmy my hips, trying to work myself out. The handlebar's pressed into my gut.

Tears slide down my face, over my lips. The taste of salt. The sensation of spinning. I'm going to be sick.

The boys are inches away now, their fingertips within reach. I lean back, reminding myself that they aren't real, that this is supposed to be fun.

Breathe through your anxiety, Dr. Donna would say.

I call up some of her other favorite sayings too—even those that don't quite fit—in an effort to stay grounded:

Remember that sometimes our minds play tricks. Sometimes what we think is real is colored by our imagination.

Allusion is temporary—our brain's way of protecting itself and processing information.

You've been through a lot, Ivy. Post-traumatic stress disorder can do that; it can impair your ability to decipher what's real from what isn't.

The boys reach toward my neck. Tears continue down my cheeks.

"Should've gotten out when you had your chance," they sing. *"Now it's time to do the dead man's dance."* They begin to dance, kicking their feet right and left, their dark eyes staring through me.

Moments later, the engine roars beneath my train cart. I creep forward again, plunging through the hologram.

The cart climbs upward, finally soaring through a loop-de-loop. The tracks screech with every turn. Finally, I can hear the hollers and cheers of the others as I go barreling down another drop.

At the end of the ride.

Outside again.

I'm able to see.

It takes me a second to realize that I'm behind Parker, rather than in front of him. Frankie and Natalie's carts are reversed as well.

"It's about time," Shayla says, shouting back at me. "We've been waiting, like, a kagillion hours for you to come out. Okay, so more like five minutes." She giggles. "We all came out at different times."

I seriously have no words. My breath's gone. I can't speak. It feels like I've been run over by a bus.

"So, what's next?" Garth asks, already looking for the next thrill.

"Hold up," Shayla says, standing up, hands on hips, clearly for the camera. "I mean, was that intense or what? A ride that goes underground? All of a sudden my train cart stopped and music began to play with a little girl's voice singing about burying a body. I recognized the song, but I couldn't remember if it was in *Night Terrors II* or *III*?"

"It was in number three," Frankie says. "The song is called 'Flatline' by Klockwise Krystina."

"It's in the scene with the postal guy at Little Sally's lemonade stand," Garth adds.

"My cart stopped too," Natalie says. "But only for a second, and there were so many sounds: a motor revving, wheels squeaking, the Nightmare Elf's laugh, and that heavy metal music."

"Not to mention your dead brother's voice," Garth says.

"Wait, what heavy metal music?" Parker asks. "All I heard was whispering. How about you?" He turns back to me.

I shake my head, unable to answer. My whole body's sweating and yet I feel completely chilled.

"So, then after that first drop," Shayla continues, "we must've all gone in different directions, and experienced different things."

While the others seem intrigued by that idea, I'm overwhelmed by it. I mean, if I thought this was hard—separating for just a handful of seconds—how am I possibly going to face the nightmare of my life on my own?

PARKER

AFTER THE TRAIN OF TERROR, WE REMAIN HANGING out by the ride, comparing one another's thrill. Ivy is way freaked out. Her eyes are red and she's visibly trembling.

"What did you actually see in there?" I ask her.

"Two boys," she says. "Dressed in tuxedos and singing a twisted version of 'Three Blind Mice.'" She takes a deep breath and then proceeds to describe a couple of kids that sound all too familiar.

"Danny and Donnie Decker from *Nightmare Elf II: Carson's Return*," Garth says, all but drooling. "Did they do the dead man's dance?"

Ivy bites her lip and gives me a blank stare, leading me to assume that she hasn't seen the movie. I wonder if she's seen any of Blake's films. And, if not, what the hell *is* she doing here?

"Man, I love those Decker boys." Garth smiles. "The scene where they sneak off from their cousin's wedding and get lost in the woods . . ."

"Only to find the Dark House," Shayla adds.

"Their nightmares about being poisoned by aliens were epic," Garth says. "Anyway, sounds like I picked the wrong cart. All I got was a fan blowing at the back of my head and the Nightmare Elf's evil giggle."

"And all *I* got were some dancing shadows and the rattle of Lizzy Greer's shopping cart," Frankie says.

I look toward Natalie, who's fallen silent, and take out my mental camera.

ANGLE ON NATALIE

She's sitting on the ground, picking at
the hair on her arm (just about the only
skin that's visible). The rest of her
is covered in clothes (long dress, high
boots, zip-up jacket, scarf, and oversize
sunglasses).

NATALIE
(catching me spying on her)
Harris won't stop talking now. He
keeps saying that it isn't safe here—
that we should find a way out.

GARTH
(to Natalie)
Just curious, but do they wear
straitjackets where you live?

Shayla cracks up in response.

FRANKIE
(rubbing his chin)
Hmm . . . I wonder if Dara would think
a comment like that is funny.

Shayla's face drops. Her eyes narrow. The
tension in the air thickens.

SHAYLA
Why would you say something like
that?

                    FRANKIE

          Oh, I don't know. Maybe it's because
          you're fake.

                    SHAYLA

          Excuse me?

          She cocks her head, as though genuinely
          confused.

                    SHAYLA (CONT'D)
          How am I fake?

                    FRANKIE

          Are you kidding?
                    (grinning)
          Where do I even begin?

                    SHAYLA

          Give me one example.

                    FRANKIE

          Well, for starters, you claim to feel
          bad about not being there for Dara,

and for just playing along when others
made fun of her. And yet it seems
you're just as insensitive now.

                    SHAYLA
Wait, where is all of this coming from?
Did I do something that hurt you?

                    FRANKIE
Forget about me. I mean, *seriously*?
You're so wrapped up in the World of
Shayla that you don't even have a
clue, do you? Think about it. Those
nightmares you have, it's like Dara's
haunting you, trying to subconsciously
get it through your head.

                    SHAYLA
Get *what* through my head? If I hurt
you, I didn't intend to.

                    FRANKIE
Forget it.
                    (laughing, tossing his hands up)

I give up.

CUT TO:

While Shayla licks her superficial wounds, and Garth and Frankie saddle up for another ride on the Nightmare Elf's Train of Terror, Ivy and I move to a bench. The temperature's dropped and I can feel her trembling. I wrap my arm around her shoulder, unable to stop thinking about last night.

It was nice spending the night with her. I close my eyes, picturing us lying together in bed, her back pressed against my chest, the scent of chocolate in the air.

"Parker?" she asks, pulling me back to PRESENT DAY: EXT. AMUSEMENT PARK—DUSK.

She nods in the direction of the ride. Garth and Frankie have squished themselves into the fifth train cart—the same one that Ivy had.

"What the hell?" Frankie shouts out, smacking at the start button.

The ride doesn't seem to be working now; nothing's happening. And the lights in the Nightmare Elf's eyes have gone out.

Ivy rests her head against my shoulder and reaches to take my hand. "Thanks for being so sweet to me."

"It's easy being sweet to you."

"It'd probably be easier hanging out with the others—having fun like them."

"I want to be with you," I say, giving her hand a squeeze.

"Good." She smiles. "Because I want to be with you, too." And I have no idea if she means for the next five minutes or the next five years, but I don't even care. Because we're together right now.

NATALIE

"WHAT'S HAPPENING TO US?" HARRIS ASKS. "I FEEL LIKE WE'RE *drifting apart.*"

"You're just angry because I'm not doing what you say. I'm not your puppet, Harris."

At first I thought it was a relief that he was talking to me again. But I have a strong suspicion that most of what Harris has been saying since his silent treatment has been a complete and utter lie, his way of getting back at me for leaving home in the first place. He doesn't normally get nasty like this. It's only happened a handful of times—and only when he's feeling particularly strong about something—that he'll punish me in the few ways he can. If it isn't silence, it's his incessant talking, especially when I'm asleep to intentionally keep me up. But I don't hold it against him. He's stuck on the other side, living in a sort of purgatory. Sometimes I wonder if he isn't waiting for me. Other times I think that if I didn't feel so alone, he'd leave me for good.

I don't expect the others to understand any of this. I know that it sounds crazy. It goes against what we've all been conditioned to believe about death.

I tried to talk about my ability to speak with Harris in one of my sessions with Dr. Gilpin. But she responded by asking if I ever thought about hurting myself, which is basically shrink-speak for, "Do you fantasize about getting up close and personal with a noose and/or razor blade, plastic bag, exhaust pipe, coat hanger, railroad track, fill in the blank with your suicide method of choice."

When I told her no, she prescribed me more pills, which I thought to be ironic considering that pills can also be ammo depending on how many you take in one sitting.

"Body lice?" Garth asks.

It takes me a moment to realize that he's directing the question at me, because I'm scouring my arms, trying to count up all the remaining hairs. I wish I had a marker with me. I wish he would mind his own business.

Though, I'll have to admit, it was kind of cool at brunch, when we were opening up about stuff, and when I told the group about Harris and my issue with mirrors. Cool . . . except for when Shayla said I'd be gorgeous beneath all my layers. Bullshit. I saw the expression on her face when she busted in on me in the bathroom door and saw my reflection. That was truth enough for me.

"Go to hell," I tell Garth. Unfortunately, the words barely come out in a whisper and he's already turned around. And I've lost count of arm hairs, which Harris finds hysterical.

I've tried to tell my parents that Harris talks to me, that he's been growing up right along with me. Every birthday I have is his birthday, too. Every holiday celebrated, every family dinner, every therapy session and test I take at school.

He's there. He doesn't leave me. It's as if his soul is alive inside of me.

Even his love of guitar. The first time I went to a concert— really an arts festival in town, where various bands came to perform—we heard this guy play an acoustic guitar. Harris got completely swept up in the beauty of it all—the notes, the rhythm, the emotion strumming from every chord. Shortly after, I asked my parents to get me an acoustic guitar. I took lessons for Harris. Kept the guitar tuned for Harris. Polished the cedarwood. Switched over to an electric when he asked. Practiced all my chords, memorized every song.

For Harris.

You'd think my parents would want to know that when our tiny bodies left the womb barely a minute apart—one of us crying and the other without breath—that we were still connected in spirit. But they won't hear any of it.

Talking to them about Harris only scores me more sessions with more therapists, more people trying to fix me.

I know it breaks Harris's heart. I know he'd do anything to be able to communicate with our parents using me as the go-between. Maybe then he'd be able to pass on. Maybe then his voice would fade.

The weird part? He doesn't normally tell me things I don't already know. Like, he'll give me his opinions, but because he never leaves me, he never reports news to me—until coming to this amusement park, that is. Ever since we got here, it's been one report after another from him about stuff he couldn't possibly know.

"I'm telling you the truth," Harris says. *"It isn't safe for you there."*

"I think you just want to ruin my time," I tell him. "You're angry, and you don't know any other way to express that anger."

"Sounds like someone's been spending too much time with shrinks."

"This ride is crap," Frankie shouts, still trying to get the Train of Terror to work.

I get up and move to stand in front of Ivy, angled away from the video camera. I hate that we're being filmed. When the

Nightmare Elf dropped that bomb, I had to hold myself back from throwing up. But then I took a deep breath, pulled out a couple of hair strands, counted up all the water bottles behind the snack shack—thirty-three, plus twelve candy apples, sixteen bags of popcorn, forty boxes of Jujyfruits—and reminded myself that I still have choices.

I can choose not to watch the film.

It doesn't have to ruin my experience here.

It's obvious that Ivy's ride on the terror train was far more terrifying than any of ours, and that it's affected her in a major way. I can't help feeling jealous of that. What I wouldn't give to get distracted by fear, to have it sneak up and give me a rush.

"Hey, Natalie," she says, looking up at me. Her brown eyes focus in and she cocks her head to the side. For just a moment I wonder if she can see straight through me all the way to Harris's soul.

"It's all going to work out fine," I tell her, recycling a phrase that's been used on me time and time again. I know the response doesn't fit, and I know the words are shit, but it's all I can think of at the moment.

Her eyes narrow; she looks confused. "Okay, but didn't you just say that we needed to get out of here?"

"Harris said that, not me," I say, correcting her. "And I think he might've been lying. When he first says stuff to me, it sounds pretty convincing inside my head, but then, after I think about it, I have to question his intentions. Like, is he really being honest? Or just trying to ruin my experience?"

Ivy's face scrunches, confused, and I'm not at all surprised. I sound like a flake, like my word can't at all be trusted, when in fact it's Harris's word that's up for debate.

"Let's keep moving," Frankie says, standing just behind us now. There's a determined look on his face. "Time's ticking and I want to go find my nightmare ride. I didn't come all this way not to meet Blake."

"I'll second that," Garth says.

"And I'll third it," Shayla agrees.

Surprisingly, Ivy follows along, and so does Parker. I fall in line too, shrouding my face as I move past the cameras, once again trying to block out Harris's voice, despite how empty I feel in his silence.

FRANKIE

WE MOVE THROUGH THE AMUSEMENT PARK, PAST ALL
sorts of games of chance. Lights flash. Bells ring. Metal music
blares.

"Step right up," a deep voice calls out. It's coming from a mannequin: Sebastian Slayer from *Forest of Fright*, dressed in his overalls
and work boots, with a pickax slung over his shoulder. He stands
in front of a bowling game with his famous toothy grin. "Hit the
pin and win, win, win. Easy as squeezy. I love bein' cheesy."

"I love being cheesy too," Garth says, giving the mannequin
a thumbs-up.

"The voice is probably motion activated," Parker says.

I'd have to agree. As soon as Shayla goes to give the mannequin a high five, we hear Sebastian's snort of a laugh, making all of us laugh too.

Garth steps up to try a game called Dead Ringer, based on a game that I've seen at practically every carnival I've ever been to. Except, instead of trying to toss a plastic ring around a glass bottle, you need to throw a miniature noose around the neck of a Barbie doll.

There's got to be at least two hundred Barbies lined up: Biker Barbie, Studious Brunette, Zombie Barbie, Princess Barbie-with-a-unicorn-on-her-head . . .

Ivy, Natalie, and Parker try the game out too, all of them grabbing nooses and tossing them into the sea of Barbie hell. Shayla, on the other hand, retreats back, her face all pouty like someone just died. Still, she makes sure to angle herself at the camera so the world can see just how tormented she is.

"My money's on Hula Girl," Garth says, trying to hook the Barbie that's wearing the floral lei and grass skirt. He doesn't succeed on the first try, nor does he succeed on the fifth, but that doesn't stop him from snagging himself a plastic sword from behind the counter as his prize.

We keep exploring, stopping for a few rounds of Forest of Fright Skee-Ball (the faces of the Targo triplets are on all of the balls), and a game of Nightmare Elf on the Shelf, where you have to knock Nightmare Elf dolls off a fireplace mantel, using Christmas stockings filled with sand.

"Step right up," Slayer says. "Hit the pin and win, win, win. Easy as squeezy. I love bein' cheesy."

"I really want to get to my ride," I say.

Shayla quickens her pace to catch up to me. "You're so brave," she tells me, trying to suck up, as if I didn't just tell her off. "I'm such a wimp when it comes to face-to-face stuff—stuff outside the safety of a movie or TV screen, I mean. And, let's face it, that's, like, the *worst* possible quality for someone who's supposed to face her biggest nightmare, right? You totally should've seen me at *La Bocca della Verità*."

"Bocci dell *what*?" I ask.

"*La Bocca della Verità*," she says again, carefully enunciating every syllable. "You know, the Mouth of Truth." She looks at me with a concerned expression, like I'm supposed to have a clue or give a shit. "You put your arm in the mouth—the sculpture of a mouth, that is—and it bites off the hands of liars. It's in Rome," she says, still trying to jog my memory, like I've ever been out of the country. "In the church of Santa Maria."

"I'll take your word for it," I say. She's so people-dumb it's scary.

Finally, we reach the back end of the park. I look up at the gate;

it's at least thirty or forty feet high. There are three video cameras pointed down at us from the network of barbed wire. While Natalie turns away from them, Garth steps right out in front.

"Who'll give me fifty bucks to flash?" he asks.

"How about fifty cents?" I offer.

"This ass has star potential." Garth undoes his pants, letting them fall to his ankles; evidently it was never a question of money. He pulls down his boxers, bends over, and shakes his hairy ass.

"Eww!" Ivy shouts.

Shayla, on the other hand, thinks it's the funniest thing ever. "Should I flash too?" she asks.

"Definitely," Garth says, drawing up his pants.

But she hops away, the tease that she is, and leads us farther into the park.

We stop to go on the Eureka Shrieker, which is sort of like the Round Up, only faster, with Eureka's screaming voice in the background, shrieking over the sound of a chain saw.

"That was crazy," Ivy says, coming out of the ride, her hand clenched over her heart. But I also catch a glimpse of a smile, so I think she kind of enjoyed it.

Meanwhile, Natalie's got a huge grin on her face, no longer talking to herself or picking at her arm hair. And Parker's explaining to Ivy who Pudgy the Clown is (basically that Pudgy's the product of Eureka Dash's nightmares).

"And Eureka Dash?" Ivy asks.

Seriously, is this chick for real?

Shayla continues to lead the way, already onto the next ride. From the outside, Hotel 9 appears to be a haunted house. A sign at the entrance asks, ARE YOU READY TO CHECK OUT?, which is basically Blake-speak for "Are you ready to die?"

We enter through a cobweb-laden door, only to discover that it isn't a haunted house at all. A giant open area has been decorated to look like the lobby of Hotel 9, in all its Gothic glory: red couches, dark walls, gold accents, and fancy mahogany furniture.

"Sweet!" Garth says.

My sentiments exactly. There are seven chair swings that hang suspended from the ceiling. We each take a seat, and the swings spin in a circle as we fly around the room.

Shayla, Garth, and Natalie extend their arms outward, making like they're birds or planes. Clips from *Hotel 9* begin to play all around us—guests screaming, dishes breaking, the chandelier crashing down in the center of the lobby as Sidney Scarcella cuts the chain with a machete.

It's absolutely epic.

"Someone looks a little green," I say, noticing Garth's sour expression as we exit the ride.

"Well if I need to barf, I'll be sure to do it on your face," he says. "Not that anyone would notice."

"That's actually pretty funny," I tell him, way too pumped to get pissed.

We pass by a fun house and then stop in front of a ride called the Wild Thing. There's a huge stuffed grizzly standing in front of it—the kind you see at lodges in the middle of nowhere.

"The bear," Garth says, lighting up like a Christmas tree. "Care to claim your pain, *now*?" He looks at Ivy.

"It isn't mine," she says.

"Ho hum, it must be Taylor's." He sighs.

The bear towers over me by at least three feet. Its mouth is wide open, exposing sharp yellow teeth and a thick gray tongue. With its arms raised, it's mid-growl, as if ready to pounce.

I reach out to touch its fur and it lets out a loud, hungry roar.

"Holy shit!" I yell, jumping back.

Ivy yells out too. But the others laugh, including Natalie, who also lets out a Sebastian Slayer–worthy snort.

I look beyond the bear, at the ride. There's a tent set up, as well as a campfire, and some lawn chairs. Behind the tent, there's a network of trees and brush, like a forest. A trail cuts through it, reminding me of the path we took behind the Dark House, when we went to look for Midge.

Garth pokes his toy sword into the grizzly's gigantic stomach. The bear lets out another roar, but Garth doesn't so much as flinch.

"Let's keep moving," Parker says.

"Not before we do the *Wild Thing*." Garth starts singing, swaying his hips, and flailing his arms. He looks like he's having a seizure.

"Ride your own wild thing," I tell him. "This one isn't yours."

"Well, aren't you a fun poker," he says, pointing the tip of the sword into my bicep—again, and again, and again. I'm tempted to tear it out of his hands, but I clench my teeth and turn away, refusing to let him get to me. We move past the Wild Thing ride and make a sharp turn. Finally, I see my nightmare. I'd recognize it anywhere.

Graveyard Dig is set back from the other rides, beyond an iron gate. There are headstones lined up in rows. Some look ancient, tilted to one side or leaning slightly backward. Others are in the shape of a cross.

There's a king-size bed in the middle of the cemetery. There's also a dresser, a night table, and a closet. It's supposed to be my parents' room.

"Is this your ride?" Shayla asks.

I nod, feeling the color drain from my face.

"Batter up," Garth says. He's absolutely loving this.

Admittedly, I'm dreading it. Standing just outside the gate, I spot a rusty mailbox beside the lock. I open the lid. The action sets off a voice—one that's slow and deep, and laced with static and clicking: "Welcome, Mr. Rice. Are you ready to dig?"

Chills ripple down my back.

Garth scoots down to check out the box, pressing his ear against the side.

"Mr. Rice?" the voice asks. "Are you ready to dig?"

"You bet," I say, trying my best to sound brave.

"Use the key inside this mailbox to unlock the gate and your closet door," the voice continues. "Take the flashlight, too. You'll need it."

"Are you okay to do this?" Shayla asks me.

I reach inside the mailbox for the key and the flashlight. "Sure," I say, looking out at the graveyard and thinking of that day, thirteen years ago, when I saw my uncle buried. I click on the flashlight, my fingers jittery.

"Good luck," Parker says.

I unlock the gate and close it up behind me. It locks automatically with a deep *clink*.

Shayla stares at me through the bars. "It'll be over before you know it." She gives me a thumbs-up and flashes me a silly smile, still trying to get back on my good side.

"Just do me a favor," I tell her. "If I don't come out in fifteen minutes, come and get me, okay?"

"What are you talking about? Of course, you'll come out."

"Just promise me," I say, remembering how I passed out at

Uncle Pete's burial. If I passed out inside this ride, who knows when I'd come to.

"I promise." She smiles, beaming like it's her birthday.

I turn away so she won't see my lip twitch any more than she already has, and then I head straight toward the closet.

Spotlights shine over the cemetery, highlighting some writing on the bed. A line's been spray-painted down the center of the mattress. On one side of it, it reads, *Mommy?*

"You're doing great," Shayla says.

I trip over something. A rock slab. I swipe the fog from in front of my eyes, but more fog fills the space. I navigate my way through it, using the flashlight to show the way. Finally, I find the closet door. It's surprisingly heavy, and I have to use both hands to unlock and open it.

I step inside. The door swings shut behind me. If I thought it was dark before, it's nothing compared to now. I try the knob; it's locked. I shine my flashlight around the perimeter of the space. The room is about the size of a small bathroom—much bigger than my parents' actual closet—but the floor is covered in carpet, just like the real deal.

In the corner, on the floor, sitting beside a shovel, a phone rings. I pick up the receiver, noticing an extra-long coil cord; it drags against the carpet. "Hello?"

"Good evening, Frankie." A male voice.

"Who is this?" I wait a couple of seconds before trying the knob again. It twists left and right, but I can't get the door to open.

I move over to the phone base and push the lever to hang up, trying to get a dial tone. The phone is dead.

I point my flashlight at the wire; the beam shakes with the tremble of my hand. The wire's stuck in a wall crack. I give the wire a tug, only to find that the end's been severed. This isn't an actual working phone. There's no real outlet. Nothing's plugged in.

The phone rings again. Four rings, five.

I pick it up, able to hear breathing—and suddenly I feel stupid. I mean, why am I bothering with the phone? And yet, I know his voice came from the receiver. I look at the earpiece. At the same moment, I hear laughter—it's coming from the receiver again, only this time it sounds farther away.

I hurl the phone at the wall, unable to think straight. The phone smashes. I position the flashlight on the ground, angled in my direction so that I can see. And then I grab the shovel, determined to bust the door open. I wedge the blade into the door crack, beside the knob. The wood makes a creaking sound, but everything remains intact. I try again, jamming the blade deeper, but still nothing gives.

After several more attempts at trying to break the lock, I toss the shovel to the ground. My flashlight beam shines over the blade.

And that's when it hits me.

I look down at the rug, remembering how, in my nightmare, I raked my fingers over the carpet, thinking that it was my uncle's plot site, convinced that there was a phone ringing inside his casket . . . my mother calling at last.

On hands and knees, I scour the rug in search of a seam, feeling my fingertips burn from the friction. At last, I find a spot where the rug's been cut. I peel away a corner section. Beneath it, there's a two-feet-by-two-feet wooden panel on the floor with a shallow metal handle. I pull up on the handle, feeling a surge of excitement.

A ladder leads underground. I grab the shovel and flashlight and begin climbing down, my adrenaline peaked. It's dark at the bottom, but there are spotlights placed about, helping me to see.

I'm in a giant underground room, dug out of the dirt—like an abandoned mine. There's a wooden frame with strapping overhead and along the walls, holding the space together, so it doesn't come caving in.

There are headstones lined up in rows with a single red rose placed at each site. Tarantula-shaped trees border the graveyard, just as I described in my essay.

I look beyond everything, trying to assess how extensive the space is—if there might be a network of underground tunnels. But the lighting only goes to the edge of the cemetery. Beyond that is total darkness.

A blue teddy bear with no mouth and only one eye—just like the one I had when I was five—sits propped against a headstone. I grab it and make my way toward the back row, where there's a gaping hole in the ground.

There are two headstones behind the hole—the only ones without roses. One of them reads PETER RICE, my uncle's name. The other stone has a skull etched into the surface. There's writing beneath the skull, only it's too small to see from this angle. I move closer and scoot down, able to see: FRANKIE RICE engraved in the granite. Below my name is my date of birth—followed by today's date.

The sight of it freaks me out.

I look down into the hole. It's at least five feet deep and eight feet long and wide. A phone rings, again. It's coming from inside the hole—buried beneath the dirt. I point my flashlight, but I can't see a phone. I crawl forward on my hands and knees, trying to get a better look. Nothing. It must be buried pretty well.

Still holding the shovel, I slide down into the hole, ignoring the tiny voice inside me that says it's going to be a bitch to climb back out. The dirt is dry and powdery around me. It crumbles like a landslide, creating a pile at the bottom.

Still focused on the ringing, I aim the blade of the shovel into the dirt, knowing what I have to do. It feels good to dig—like in some weird-fantastical-surreal sort of way, I've been given a second chance to answer the call I missed thirteen years ago, when I couldn't wake up from my nightmare. What awaits me on the other end of that line?

My forehead is sweating. The muscles in my shoulders ache as I get deeper into the hole, on one hand driven by the ringing, on the other hand maddened by it. It's getting louder with each shovelful of dirt. I dig faster, sweat dripping from my forehead. About eight feet deep now, a dusting of dirt gets into my eyes. I drop the shovel to wipe my face.

At the same instant, I hear it. A clamoring sound: metal hitting something hard. My eyes stinging with dirt, I grab the shovel and continue to dig, finally finding the source.

A dark mahogany casket. The phone must be inside it. With trembling fingers, I dust it off and open it up. The hinges whine.

There's the phone.

There's Uncle Pete: a skeleton lying on a bed of creamy satin, dressed in a navy blue suit and a red tie. There's a watch around the skeleton's wrist. The strap is braided like his actual one. I slip the watch off and turn it over in my hand, feeling its weight. The back is blank, unlike my uncle's, which was engraved. The difference is reassuring, but still I feel like I'm going to be sick.

The phone rings and rings. It's tucked beneath Uncle Pete's arm. I pick it up and click on the receiver. "Hello?" I answer.

"Did you find your teddy bear?" a woman's voice asks.

"I did," I say, looking around for it.

"You'll always be my special boy," she says. "Frankie and Mom. Mom and Frankie."

Mom. The word has become somewhat foreign to me over the years. It feels weird to hear it directed at me now.

"Why did you leave?" I ask, unable to help myself.

There's silence for a moment as I wait for her response.

"Did you find your teddy bear?" she asks again.

I search around some more, inside the hole. No bear. "I must've left it above . . . outside, I mean. Should I get it?"

"You'll always be my special boy. Frankie and Mom. Mom and Frankie."

The receiver still gripped in my hand, I scurry to climb upward, out of the hole, to get to the bear. The dirt is powdery and light. The walls break apart beneath my grip and I fall to my feet.

I jump up, using the pile of dirt as leverage.

My fingers graze the top of the hole. Still holding the phone, I try to struggle up farther, but then something in my shoulder pops. A throbbing ache. My bicep quivers. I slide down again.

I get up and plunge my foot into the wall, but I can't get a good foundation. My foot falls away as the dirt slides down.

"Help!" I shout. The phone slips from my grip. I scramble to pick it up. A dial tone plays.

My one-eyed bear comes flying into the hole, landing on Uncle Pete. I can see a network of wiring above, just beneath the wood-strapped ceiling. A spotlight shines over it all, giving me a view of a pulley system. A giant bucket inches across it. Someone must be up there.

"Hello?" I call out.

The bucket wobbles from side to side and then turns over completely. Dirt comes raining down—on top of my head, surrounding my body. I try to wade through it as I struggle to get back on the wall, to work my way to the top. But the pulley continues to crank forward and soon another bucket appears. Fresh dirt comes pouring in, knocking me down against the coffin. I fall to my knees.

"Wait!" I shout. "I need help. Someone get me out of here!"

The skeleton's covered now. Dirt gets in my mouth, my eyes, my nostrils, my ears. The dial tone turns into an off-the-hook buzz, and then it becomes muffled by dirt as more of it comes piling in.

I crawl out from a heap. For just a moment, I think I've got a solid grip on the wall, only to realize that it's the floor. I'm turned around, upside down, unable to see, completely in a panic.

Just then, I hear someone running. I can't tell where it's coming from—if it's above or below me.

More dirt comes, weighing me down. Lying on my stomach, I struggle to turn over. But it's like a giant pig pile with me at the bottom. I can't move. I can hardly breathe. *Please*, I pray inside my head.

I don't want to open my mouth. It's already full of dirt. I try to move my leg, but there's too much weight on top of my limbs. And still I feel more dirt coming down. *Please*, I pray some more, but I'm not sure if anyone's listening.

The last thing I hear is the muffled laughter of the Nightmare Elf.

Giggle.

Giggle.

Giggle.

SHAYLA

I COULD TELL THAT FRANKIE WAS ANXIOUS. HIS LIP started twitching and his face lost all color. I'm feeling anxious too. I haven't been to a cemetery since Dara died, and Frankie's Graveyard Dig is bringing me back to that day.

I remember how people kept coming up to me: Dara's parents, her relatives, teachers, mutual friends, those I didn't know, faces I'd never seen before. They offered tissues, a place to sit, shoulders to cry on, someone to talk to.

"You were her one and only true friend. Please, Shayla-honey, you have my number; feel free to use it."

"You must be devastated to have lost such a close friend. You two were like inseparable sisters."

"Please, Shay-Shay, if you need anything, don't hesitate to ask."

Their kindness was too much to bear, but I didn't deserve any of it, and I wanted to feel all of it—all the pain, every bit of the heartache.

What Frankie doesn't know is that I *am* affected by her death. And that I *do* feel bad about the way things played out. My nightmares don't need to tell me anything, because deep down I already know. Deep down I've always known. I wasn't a true friend, but that didn't mean she had to die. And it doesn't make me responsible for her death. As guilty as I sometimes feel.

I could see Dara slipping deeper into depression, spending more of her time alone. I thought that maybe I could be friends with her in secret, when nobody else was around. But then Dara's parents announced that they were getting a divorce and she needed me full-time. Even though my heart told me otherwise, I wouldn't make myself available to her, except for when it was socially safe. Obviously no one at Dara's funeral had been aware of any of that, otherwise they wouldn't have bothered with me.

The fog in the graveyard is thick, making it impossible to keep track of Frankie. "I promise," I call out again, hoping that he hears me.

I'd made a promise to Dara, too. Just before she transferred to my school, over hot fudge sundaes with candy canes sticking out, we made a whipped-cream-with-maraschino-cherries vow to always be there for each other, no matter what.

Parker peers through the bars. "Frankie, how's it going?" He squints hard, trying to see through the clouds of fog.

But Frankie doesn't answer. There's a deep *thwack* sound, like something heavy hitting against a slab of wood.

"He must be inside that shed," Ivy says.

I look around at the headstones, wondering what this ride could possibly be—maybe a mind challenge of some sort or an underground haunted house. I pull up on the lid of the mailbox, half expecting a voice to say something, but it remains silent.

Ten minutes later and I'm feeling completely restless. Natalie and Garth appear to be restless too. While she paces back and forth, Garth won't stop squawking about his growling stomach.

"I gotta eat," he says, finally heading off to find food.

I walk around the perimeter of the gate to where Ivy and Parker now stand, on the other side of the ride. The back of the shed is in full view. "Frankie?" I call.

A moment later, there's a ringing sound, like someone's phone. It's followed by music from *The Wizard of Oz*. "Ding dong! The witch is dead!" Only the music isn't coming from the graveyard.

I turn to look out into the park. Garth is at the nearby snack shack. Amusement park rides continue to bing, blink, and blare—only none of the sounds seems to match the *Wizard of Oz* tune.

"Where's it coming from?" Parker asks.

Ivy takes her bag from around her shoulder and holds it up to her ear. "Here." She squats down, dumping the entire contents of her purse onto the ground. But still there's nothing to explain the sound.

She fishes inside an interior pocket, finally finding the source. A cell phone. With a leopard-print cover.

"It's Taylor's," Ivy says. "I forgot that I shoved it in here."

"Well, answer it." I squat down beside her.

Ivy clicks the phone on. "Hello?" she says, switching over to speakerphone mode.

"Who is this?" a female voice asks.

"Ivy. I mean, that's my name . . . Ivy . . . Jensen." Ivy makes a face, realizing that she's not exactly killing it on this call.

I hold out my hand, silently offering to take the phone from her.

But then: "How did you end up with my cell phone, Ivy?" the girl asks.

"Taylor?" Ivy's eyes widen with alarm.

"Yes."

"You left it," Ivy says; her hand begins to tremble. "When

you went for a walk . . . you left it behind, in our room. I'm your roommate for the weekend—at least, I was supposed to be."

"Except I didn't go for a walk, Ivy. Please tell me that you aren't at the Dark House right now."

"I'm not," Ivy says, locking eyes with me. "We're at an amusement park."

A couple of seconds later, Garth approaches, holding a piece of fried dough. He takes a giant bite. "Shit, this crap is cold," he says, spitting it out for the camera's sake.

I shush him, nodding to the phone, and Parker pulls him out of earshot. Meanwhile, Ivy is on the verge of panic. Her chin quivers. There are hives all over her neck.

"Who brought you to the amusement park?" Taylor asks. "Is it part of the contest? Are you alone or are others with you?"

"Where are *you*?" Ivy asks. Her phone-holding hand continues to shake.

"If the park is part of the contest," Taylor says, "then you're in serious danger."

"Wait, *what*?" Ivy's face goes flush. Her breath starts to quicken. Her eyes widen and her face is flushed. She looks like she's going to faint.

I grab the phone from her.

"Listen to me," Taylor continues. "Get out—*now*. If it isn't already too late. Didn't you get my message?"

I click off the speakerphone option and stand up. "What message? The one in the closet or—"

Before I can get the latter question out, Taylor is already talking. But there's another voice too. Maybe there's a crossed line, or maybe Taylor isn't alone. There's static on the phone, making it hard to hear.

I move away, searching for the hotspot, blocking my free ear.

"Do whatever you can," she tells me.

"Whatever I can to *what*?" I attempt to ask, but only part of the question goes through. The call is dropped.

"Crap!" I shout.

I start to look up the recent calls when I hear a banging sound come from the graveyard. "Frankie," I say, my voice barely audible. I look at my watch. It's been twenty minutes now and he still isn't out.

And I've broken yet another promise.

GARTH

FRANKIE'S BEEN INSIDE HIS NIGHTMARE RIDE FOR A while, which tells me that it must be pretty decent. Meanwhile, everybody's freaking out, including Parker, who tries to explain why I should give a shit that Taylor called her own cell phone.

"Seriously?" I ask him. "The only thing I give a shit about where Taylor's concerned is the fact that Ivy broke the rules by smuggling Taylor's cell phone in here. We better not be penalized for it." I look out at the park. It's dark out now and the glowing lights are mesmerizing.

"I think it's high time we go look for one of those emergency phones," Ivy says.

"Except there are no emergency phones." Natalie blocks her ears, as if she's concentrating on what's being said inside that screwy head of hers. The girl is such a fake. "Harris says that the Nightmare Elf was lying about the phones."

"I'll go check things out." Parker heads out into the park, donning his invisible bright red cape and superhero onesie.

"Now what?" Shayla looks down at Taylor's cell phone, clenched in her hand.

"Now we check out the goods. Any compromising photos loaded on there?" I ask.

She glares at me, like I'm the biggest asshole ever, which comes as a major relief. I'd rather she think of me as an asshole than as someone who's all about his feelings.

"Ever think that maybe the phone's been rigged," I suggest. "By the mastermind himself. My money's on Taylor's nonexistence. I'll bet she's not even real—just a bogus hoax to get us all worked up."

"But I met her," Natalie says. "We were on the same flight. We rode in the same car. She talked to me."

"Sure, Scarecrow. Just like your dead brother talks to you too. Nice look, by the way," I say, referring to her hood, scarf, and sunglasses. "Do you really think this crazy act of yours is going to score you more attention from Blake?"

"I'm not looking for extra attention," she says. "If I could, I'd hide from everyone."

"Well, I really wish you would," I tell her.

"Back off," Ivy says, shooting me a dirty look. Happily, I've made another fan.

"Don't be surprised if the phone miraculously starts working again," I say. "If so-called Taylor happens to call us back at some opportune time. Remember in *Nightmare Elf IV* when Eureka's walkie-talkie only seemed to work when she was alone? It was all so plotted."

"Oh, and PS," Shayla says. "Frankie still isn't out yet, and it's been thirty minutes since he entered the graveyard."

"Which means that Blake didn't cheap out on the rides," I say. "Frankie must be getting his money's worth, so to speak."

Shayla shakes her head at me—the same way my father does when he's looking at me like I'm dirt, which is pretty much a daily occurrence.

"If you wanted *Mary Poppins*, then you picked the wrong contest," I tell them. "You came here to be scared, remember? You do something stupid—like using the emergency phone to bring the hearse back—and you risk ruining this whole thing."

"I think I'll take my chances," Ivy says.

While she and Shayla head off to the supposed hotspot, and Natalie takes a seat on the ground, engaged in a full-on conversation with herself, I look back at the graveyard, jealous that Frankie gets all the fun.

IVY

SHAYLA AND I SIT ON THE GROUND, TRYING TO GET
Taylor's phone to work.

"There's still no reception," Shayla says, "which is totally BS.
I mean, you were right here when it rang." She holds the phone
up to see if that might help, and then removes the battery and
snaps it back into place two seconds later. "The phone itself is
working fine."

"Well, maybe Garth was right. Maybe the phone's been
rigged."

"The last call received was from the nine-five-two area code," she says, looking at the phone screen.

"Is that near here?" I ask.

"Do I look like a walking Google search box? Maybe there's some clue in her pics."

I gaze over Shayla's shoulder as she searches Taylor's photo album. The same girl keeps appearing in each of the pictures, and so I assume that it's her. Taylor is really cute, with tousled blond hair like she just came from the beach, bright blue eyes, and delicate features. There are photos of her performing in plays, making goofy faces at the camera, and dancing at various recitals.

"I have to assume that she saw something at the Dark House," I say, "something that really freaked her out, because she left so abruptly, mid-unpacking, not even with her cell phone."

"So, you don't *really* think the phone's been rigged."

"All I know is that I wasn't even going to bring the cell phone with me," I tell her. "I'd slipped it into my bag, thinking that we might meet up with Taylor at some point. But the organizers didn't know that—that I'd bring it with me, that is; that I'd forget it was in my bag when we were depositing all our cell phones at the gate. They didn't even know that I'd find the phone to begin with—that I'd just happen to lie back on Taylor's bed and brush my hand against the covers in the right way. Don't you think that if they'd wanted us to find her phone, it would've been planted in a more obvious way?"

Shayla looks at her watch. "It's been forty minutes for Frankie." She tosses me the phone and then moves back over to the gate. "One of us needs to go in there," she says.

"'Not I,' said the fly," Garth says, between bites of sourdough pretzel.

"I don't want to go either," Natalie says, pausing from mumbling to herself.

"Then I'll go," Shayla says. "Somebody give me a lift."

"And what about the movie?" Garth asks her. "Or meeting Justin Blake?"

"I know." She nods. "But I promised Frankie that after fifteen minutes if he still hadn't come out, I'd go looking for him."

"Looks like you're twenty-five minutes late. So, why not make it an hour?" Garth laughs.

For once, Shayla doesn't laugh along with him. "I need to go in there," she insists.

"For all we know, Frankie's ride is already over," Garth says. "If he went underground, the exit could be anywhere—at any part of the park."

I look out at the park. A movie plays in the distance. A guy wearing a clown mask appears on the screen. He's got a girl cornered. It's nighttime and raining out. The girl melts down against a wall, begging him not to hurt her. But he sticks his knife in anyway. Her eyes bug open in shock, and then go completely vacant as her body falls limp.

Is that how my parents looked too?

"You're totally blowing it," Garth says, talking to Shayla's back.

Standing on two milk crates, she's climbed the graveyard gate and has her foot propped up on the top rung. She teeters there, trying to keep her balance.

"Are you sure you want to do this?" I ask her.

"More than sure." She jumps over. Her feet hit the ground with a thud, releasing a dusting of dirt into the air. She heads straight for the shed.

"That's it," Garth declares. "I'm done."

"With what?" I ask.

"With all of you, wasting our time, breaking the rules, and screwing everything up."

The fog machine has kicked into gear, shrouding Shayla's torso and feet, making her appear even farther away. "It's just hard to know what to believe," I tell him. "What's real versus what's screwing with our minds."

"That's the beauty of Justin Blake's work. And this is the chance of a lifetime. I don't know about any of you, but opportunities like this don't normally happen in my world. In *my* world, all anyone ever expects is failure. But Justin Blake sees more to me than that, so I'm not going to disappoint him."

I bite my lip, able to hear the angst in his voice. I can tell he really wants this. But what I want is to go home. I look back out at Shayla. She's standing just outside the shed, but I can barely even see her.

"Harris says it's too late for her," Natalie mutters, peeking through the bars. "He says it doesn't even matter if she turns back now, because she already broke the rules."

"And what does he think that means?" I ask, still on the fence about her sanity.

"Twenty-six," she says, confidence in her voice. "Twelve rectangles, four ovals, seven crosses, and three squares."

"Excuse me?" I ask her.

Tears drip from the corners of her eyes, mixing with her thick black liner and making track marks down her cheeks. "Harris says there will soon be twenty-eight. And then thirty. And probably more. And probably more rectangles. All of them with roses. Except for two that have been freshly dug out."

"Okay, you're not making any sense."

"*No!*" she shouts, but she isn't talking to me. She covers over her ears, as if lost inside her head. "That isn't true," she continues. "Don't say those things; it's all just lies."

"This whole Harris act is getting old." Garth yawns. "And so is all the bullshit drama. I'm out of here."

"Where are you going?" I ask.

The graveyard looks eerily vacant now. The fog machine has stopped again. A few residual clouds hover around the bed and dresser, but there's no sign of Frankie or Shayla. And Parker still isn't back yet.

"You're a smart girl. You can figure it out." And with that, Garth turns on his heel, leaving us in the dust.

PARKER

FADE IN:

EXT. AMUSEMENT PARK—NIGHT

ANGLE ON ME

I pass by a row of carnival games. It's dark.
The park looks nearly vacant. The blinking
game lights, coupled with their binging-
ringing sound effects, permeate the stillness.

I'm about halfway around the entrance gate and still haven't been able to find a phone, which is really sort of ridiculous considering that they've supposedly been placed for emergency purposes.

I turn a corner, passing by more games. And that's when I finally see it:

CLOSE ON AN ENGLISH PHONE BOOTH

It's about eight feet tall and three feet wide. A checkerboard of windows forms the front door panel.

I grab the handle. Lights start flashing right away, forming a frame around eight Nightmare Elf heads attached to the back wall.

There is no phone.

All the heads are the same: the Nightmare Elf with his pointed ears, Santa-like hat, and chubby face. But all the facial expressions are different: one happy, another sad. There's also a scowl, a glare, and a puckering pair of lips.

VOICE RECORDING
Ring-a-ling-ding. Throw the ring for a chance to ding-a-ling.

Is "a chance to ding-a-ling" carnival-speak for a chance to use the phone? There's a stack of plastic rings at the bottom of the booth. I grab a bunch and stand behind a designated line on the ground.

I toss a ring at one of the heads. It catches on a hat but then falls to the ground.

VOICE RECORDING
Remember, if at first you don't succeed, ring, ring again.

I toss another ring. This time it hooks around the Nightmare Elf with the happy

smile. A bell CHIMES, announcing that I've
won. I wait for something to happen, hoping
that a phone will suddenly appear.

Instead the lights go out. The ride goes
quiet. I linger a few more seconds before
chucking the rest of the rings to the ground.

I'm just about to turn away, when I spot it,
out of the corner of my eye.

CLOSE ON ELF THAT WAS FROWNING BEFORE

It now has a wild expression. Its eyes are
wide; they stare straight out into space.
Its brows are darted, and it's baring razor-
sharp teeth.

I look up at an overhead camera.

                    ME
              (shouting at the camera)
         You think this is funny?

The elf doesn't move, nor does it blink.

I move around to the back of the booth. There's a metal closet attached to the rear panel. Someone must be hiding inside that space.

                    ME
        Come out!

I kick at the metal sides and slam my fists into the back panel. When still nothing happens, I go around to the front again.

The elf's face remains with its wild expression. I study it a few seconds: its bright blue eyes, its waxy lips, its stupid rosy cheeks.

PULLBACK TO REVEAL ME

I slam the door—so hard that the glass pane BREAKS. I look back up at the camera.

                         ME

        In case you haven't already figured
        it out, I don't give a shit about
        being in your stupid film. Cut my
        role right now. I don't need this
        crap. I don't need to meet you.

I wait for something to happen or someone
to come out. When nothing and no one do, I
head back to Frankie's ride.

CUT TO: NATALIE AND IVY, EXTERIOR GRAVEYARD
DIG.

NATALIE

"WHERE ARE THE OTHERS?" PARKER ASKS.

Ivy nods to the graveyard ride. "Shayla went to look for Frankie. And Garth took off, tired of waiting around."

Parker checks his watch. A look of concern crosses his face.

"Did you find a phone?" Ivy asks him.

"Negative."

"So that was a lie," she says.

"Or maybe not," I argue. "Maybe whoever was left in charge of installing emergency phones never got around to it."

"You don't seriously believe that, do you?" he asks.

Do I? I can feel the confusion on my face. It must be catching, because Parker looks confused now too.

I move to sit on a patch of grass—away from their voices, so I won't be influenced. I close my eyes and try to concentrate on only one voice: mine. Except it's hard to know what I want, or what to think, when those things have always been dictated for me. Add that to the fact that Harris continues to tell me things he couldn't possibly know—about Frankie being buried and a blue teddy bear with a missing mouth—and it's hard to focus on the tiny voice inside of me.

In the end, I think Garth's voice is the most logical: we've all been given an opportunity here. It'd be foolish to throw it away.

I look over at Parker and Ivy, engrossed in conversation. "I finally know what I think," I say, moving to stand in front of them.

"Okay . . ." Parker still looks confused, his face twisted into a question mark.

"We need to find a way out of here," Ivy says.

"Without the others?" I ask.

"We haven't really gotten that far yet," she says.

"So, I guess you've decided to go with Harris's voice, then."

"That's right," Ivy says; her tone has softened. "I think Harris might be onto something."

"And I think he's trying to ruin our time here."

"And so what do you suggest we do?" she asks.

"Let's go on the rides," I say, feeling empowered to voice what *I* want. "We're here, so let's enjoy ourselves. Let's take advantage of this once-in-a-lifetime opportunity. Maybe we can try that terror train ride again—the one that goes underground. Maybe we can connect with Frankie and Shayla somewhere."

"We were thinking about that, too," Parker says. "But I'm not so sure we want to get lost in a web of underground tunnels."

"Especially in light of Taylor's phone call," Ivy adds.

"Didn't you listen to any of what Garth was saying? We're *supposed* to be afraid. This is *supposed* to be scary. We're at a horror-themed amusement park, where someone's filming a movie."

"I know." Ivy sighs.

"Then *what*?" I look out at the park, feeling slightly reassured that I'm not the only one who gets confused. The blinking yellow lights are nearly intoxicating, as is the smell of candy and popcorn. "Here," I say, pulling a long gray scarf from my bag. I hand it to Ivy, along with a spare pair of sunglasses. "I always keep extra stuff like this, just in case."

"What's it for?" she asks.

"Harris says you don't want to be recognized on film. Is that true? Are you already famous or something?"

Ivy's voice is gone now too.

"I don't want to be filmed either," I continue. "But I'll do just about anything to meet Justin Blake. So, I guess I'll see you guys later?" I turn away before they can respond, ready to go find my nightmare.

SHAYLA

LUCKILY, THE DOOR TO THE GRAVEYARD SHED IS
open. I go inside, and the door swings shut behind me. I try the
knob. It's locked.

"Frankie?" I call out, telling myself not to panic.

A lantern on the floor lights up the interior: wood-paneled
walls and a carpeted floor. There's nothing else in here.

I pick up the lantern, spotting a cardboard tag attached to the
handle with string. I flip the tag over, surprised to find my name
printed across it. This lantern was placed here for me. Someone

must've had another way to come in here. I search the walls and the floor, knowing there has to be a hidden door somewhere.

At last, I find it—an area where the carpet's been cut away. Beneath it is a trapdoor. Someone's tagged it as well. *Welcome, Shayla* has been spray-painted across it. I touch one of the letters and a fresh smear of black comes away on my finger.

There's a small metal handle attached to the wood. I pull up on it. A ladder leads underground. I bring the lantern closer, trying to see what's down there, but it's too dark to tell.

"Frankie?" I shout. I look back at the door. Fog begins to seep in through the crack at the bottom. Part of me is tempted to pound on the door in hopes that the others will come get me out. But I begin down the ladder anyway.

Two rungs from the bottom, a bang crashes above. I startle and look upward. The trapdoor is still open.

"Hello?" I call out. "Frankie?"

No one answers.

I hurry back up the ladder, but before I can get to the top, the trapdoor slams shut. I push on it, but it won't budge.

I take a deep breath in an effort to quell the jangling nerves inside me. *What can this moment teach me?* I repeat inside my head—one of my yoga master's many life mantras.

I begin down the ladder again, also thankful for Garth's

logic: I've come here to be scared. I knew that when I signed up. Breathe in, breathe out. Remember that things are as they should be. There's no reason to panic.

Once I've reached the bottom of the ladder, I turn around, hoping to see Frankie. But there's nobody else here, and it seems I've reached yet another graveyard. Still, the whole scene is almost enchanting—in a Gothic, medieval-looking sort of way. It reminds me of a light show that my parents took me to in Scotland when I was twelve. There are dark trees with outstretched arms and twisted boughs surrounding the perimeter. Spotlights have been strategically placed on several of the limbs, illuminating the entire area and making everything look all aglow.

Just like outside, there are rows and rows of headstones— crosses, squares, and oval ones. Each stone has a single red rose lying in front of it, except for two stones in the back.

I meander around, recognizing most of the names on the headstones. They're characters from Justin Blake's films: Farrah Noyes from *Nightmare Elf II: Carson's Return;* Darcie Scarcella from *Hotel 9: Blocked Rooms;* Josie, Carl, and Diana Baker from the original *Night Terrors*—none of them lucky enough to make it into the next movie of their series.

I move to the last row—to the two stones without roses. I check the name on the larger stone—PETER RICE—unable to place it. Perhaps he's a character from one of Blake's earlier, lesser-known films. It seems that the two stones have the same plot site, leading me to assume that there's a crypt under there, which is actually quite appropriate considering that one of the occupant's names is Peter. Perhaps Blake was paying homage to Saint Peter, buried at Old Saint Peter's Basilica in Rome.

The plot area has been freshly filled. The dirt is darker, the mound is fuller, and there's zero growth (in this case, fake grass) sprouting from the site.

A skull is etched into the granite surface of Peter's sister stone; below it is writing, only the lettering is much smaller than that of the other stones. I scoot down to get a better look, hoping to find another message or maybe a clue as to where Frankie is.

The breeze rustles through the trees; making the wind chimes clink. The sounds help ease my nerves. *I'm being watched. I'm not alone. This isn't real. This whole scene has been created for the movie.*

I move the lantern close to the smooth polished surface of the stone, able to see Frankie's name with what I assume is his birthday and today's date. I blink a couple of times, knowing that this was done for cinematic purposes. But still my stomach twists, because the gravestone looks really real, really legit.

I struggle to my feet, spotting a shovel propped against the back of the stone. My heart tightens and I take another breath, wondering if I should start digging at Frankie's site, if that's what I'm supposed to do—if it's indeed part of this nightmare-challenge, especially with a name like Graveyard Dig.

I go to grab the shovel. But then I hear something. A crunching noise. It's coming from behind the graveyard border. I can't really see back there; there aren't any lights beyond this last row of stones, but I can tell that the space continues. The wood framing overhead extends into the darkness.

"Frankie?" I call.

More crunching; it's followed by a clanking sound. Keeping a firm grip on the lantern, I move in the direction of the noises.

With the lantern's glow, I'm able to see about five feet in front of me. There's a tunnel and a gravel-lined pathway. The sides of the tunnel are made of dirt, held in place by wooden strapping. Was this once a mine?

I call Frankie's name over and over, continuing through the tunnel. I recite the Gayatri Mantra from yoga class, still trying to hold it together.

I turn to look back, but there's only blackness now. The lights by the graveyard have all been turned off.

Another noise makes me jump: the shifting of gravel. Someone's moving in my direction.

"Hello?" I hold my lantern high.

A door creaks open somewhere in front of me.

"Shay-la?" a woman sings.

I don't move. I can hardly breathe.

"Come and find me," the voice continues.

My heart is pumping furiously. My hands are shaking uncontrollably. I'm here to be scared, I remind myself.

There's a trickling sound now, like water leaking from an overhead pipe. I walk deeper into the tunnel, able to hear a tiny whimper before realizing that it's mine.

"Do you remember our promise?" the voice asks.

I stop. This is part of my contest entry.

"You said you'd always be there for me," she says.

The voice doesn't even sound like Dara's. But whoever this is clearly represents her—or at least her memory—and I suppose that's why I'm here: to face Dara once and for all.

"Are you there?" she asks.

I begin moving forward again. A knocking sound goes straight to my heart. It sounds as if someone's rapping on a door. Maybe I'm supposed to answer.

Keeping the lantern high, I search the walls as the knocking becomes louder and more desperate, as if someone's trying to get out.

"Frankie?" I shout, wondering if it might be him.

Finally, I find a large gray door. The knocking comes from the other side of it. "Hello?" I call, looking down both ends of the tunnel—from where I came and to where I'm headed. Still, there's only blackness.

I wrap my hand around the knob, hesitating to open the door, half hoping that it's locked. But the knob turns without a hitch. The door creaks open. The air through my lungs stops.

It's dark inside. I lift my lantern higher. A light turns on—from the motion of the door—and I'm able to see.

A girl. A body. Hanging inside the closet. She's dressed in a long T-shirt and heart-patterned socks; her hair is in a sideways braid.

I drop the lantern. My hands fly up to my face. It can't possibly be real. The chalky lips, the dark eyelids, the bluish-gray skin. Telephone wire is wrapped around the neck, creating a makeshift noose. The wire is attached to a light fixture. A lightbulb hangs down from the closet's ceiling.

My head feels woozy and the tunnel starts to tilt. The body wavers too. Maybe the motion of the door disturbed it.

There's something in one of the hands. An envelope. A note for me. It's stuck to the skin with double-sided tape.

I take and open it, my mind unable to catch up to the written words: *You broke our promise.*

I step back, stumbling over my feet, wanting to get away, desperate to get back to the others.

The eyes snap open. And stare back at me. Dara's pale blue eyes, crying bloodred tears.

A scream tears out my throat. I back up more—away from the door, away from her, bumping into something behind me.

A red suit. Elf boots. A person is there. Wearing gloves, his fingers wrap around my throat.

"Your role has been cut, Ms. Belmont," he says. I can feel his breath against my neck.

His fingers tighten.

I try to let out another scream, but it sounds more like a wheeze. I'm choking. His fingers press against my throat. His hands wrap around my neck.

My feet are dangling now. I picture those heart-patterned socks.

My world darkens and swirls. More creaking sounds in the distance. It's mingled with another sound, another voice.

Dara's voice. Inside my head. She's crying out to me, thanking me for being there for her. At last.

GARTH

IT TAKES ME TWO LOOPS AROUND THE PARK BEFORE I finally find my ride. It's called Nightmare Alley, which makes perfect sense, seeing as part of my childhood nightmares involved walking down a long dark alleyway in the middle of the night, with Justin Blake's characters stalking after me.

The ride itself appears to be inside a building of sorts. Four giant walls have been erected, most likely to conceal what lurks behind them. I go inside and it's like I've died and gone to nightmare heaven. I'm in an entryway with walls that are at least ten feet high. They're decorated with illustrated murals of some of Blake's most well-known characters: the Nightmare Elf holding his sack of tricks; Lizzy Greer pushing a shopping cart and swinging her bloodstained ax; Little Sally Jacobs with the skeleton keys punctured through her eyes; and Sidney Scarcella from *Hotel 9*, serving a platter full of victims' ears—to name just a few. Word bubbles blow out each of their mouths: "If you dare." "Come play with me." "Ready to check in?" They urge me farther inside.

There's a bright red door in front of me. It's shaped like the silhouette of the Dark House. I open it, and the Nightmare Elf's mischievous giggle greets me.

It's dim inside. There are streetlights strategically placed down the long narrow alleyway—just far enough away from one another to keep the creepy quotient high. Bordering the alley are buildings and shops. I can tell they're all movie-set fake, assembled for the sole purpose of my nightmare, which makes this whole experience even more incredible than it is. I mean, if it wasn't cool enough that Justin Blake created this "ride," he created it just *for me*.

I close the door, and once again I hear the Nightmare Elf's giggle. *"Come out, come out, wherever you are,"* I sing, thinking how this whole scene reminds me a little of *Sesame Street*, but for horror lovers.

There's a handful of thumbtacks scattered on the ground. I know they must've been tossed there by him, up to his corny elf trickery.

"Hey there, Darthy Garthy," the Nightmare Elf says. "Have you come to play?" The voice sounds just like it did in the movies, just like a little kid's. "*Garthy, Garthy, Go Barthy, Banana-fana Foe Farthy, Me My Mo Marthy, Garthy.*"

I continue down the alleyway. Brick buildings sandwich me in on both sides. "What are you hiding for?" I ask him. "Come out here and get me."

Instead of showing himself, the elf continues to sing: "*I know your nightmare. I took it from your sleep. And whether or not you like it, it's mine, and mine to keep.*"

I keep moving forward, spotting someone's foot sticking out from behind a Dumpster. A kid's shoe: bright red, shiny leather.

I inch closer, able to see that the shoe belongs to a girl. It's a hologram of Little Sally Jacobs from *Night Terrors*. I recognize her dark red pigtails.

Wearing striped socks and a purple dress, she's playing a game of jacks. She bounces a tiny ball and then snatches up a handful of the star-shaped pieces. There are droplets of blood on the pavement.

"Have you come to play?" she asks, keeping her face focused downward.

I open my mouth, shockingly at a loss for words.

Thankfully she fills in the blanks. "Did you bring me a piece of candy?"

I smirk, remembering how, in the movie, she was always looking for candy from strangers.

She starts singing to herself—that *"Frère Jacques"* song—and bouncing that stupid red ball of hers, collecting more jacks.

"No *parlez-vous français*," I tell her.

The jacks fall from her grip. The ball bounces away. Finally, she looks up. As expected, there are skeleton keys jabbed into the center of her eyes. Tracks of blood trickle down her cheeks. She goes to pull one of the keys out. The pulling makes a thick slopping-sucking sound.

I take a step back, bumping into a trash can.

The key is out of her eye now. "Want to play?" she asks. There's a happy smile across her face. Her lips and teeth are stained red. She stands and comes at me with the key, pushing it toward my face. *"Pansy, pretty girl, crybaby, sweet pea."*

A motor starts up behind me. I turn to look.

It's Pudgy the Clown wielding his chain saw. "Have you come to play?" he asks, giving the motor a rev. He comes right at me. His blade cuts across my neck.

I jump back, my heart pounding. I touch my neck. There is no blood.

It takes me a second to realize that the image is on a TV screen. It's three-dimensional and looks so real.

I move away, down the alley. Eureka Dash from the Nightmare Elf movies appears on the wall to my left. She's trembling; her hands shake. "He's going to come after us," she cries, tears dripping down her face.

On the other side of me, Sebastian Slayer from *Forest of Fright* is playing a piano in the middle of the forest. A severed hand and foot rest on top of the piano, right beside his pickax. He pauses from playing to look in my direction. "It's your turn next."

I want to think it's funny, but instead it makes me cringe.

A hologram of Emma Corwin from *Hotel 9: Enjoy Your Stay* is a few steps away. Using the blood from her self-sliced wrists, she starts to write *help* on the wall.

I stop, spotting something moving in the shadows, behind a Dumpster. Someone dressed up as the Nightmare Elf is slumped over Lizzy Greer's shopping cart. I approach him slowly, noticing the nightmare sack on the bottom rack of the cart.

Keeping his back to me, he asks, "Do you have any spare change?" à la Lizzy Greer.

The cart is filled up with soda cans. I know what's probably hidden among them—what Lizzy keeps tucked away.

"Spare change?" he asks again, without looking in my direction.

I start to move past him, but he pulls Lizzy's ax from the mound of cans and holds it up for show.

I take a moment to study him, wondering if he might be one of the drivers, but aside from his eyes, his face is completely covered with the elf mask.

Wearing his bright green gloves, he takes a cantaloupe from the carriage, sets it on top of the Dumpster, and chops it in two. The blade drips with juice and pulp. Cantaloupe guts plop onto the ground. "Enjoying your time at the park, so far?"

My pulse racing, I continue down the alleyway, able to feel his eyes burning into my back.

"Not so fast," he says.

I stop. And peer over my shoulder. Standing feet away, he straightens all the way up, and then comes at me with the ax. The blade slices through the air, missing my midsection by an inch, but still he manages to get my jacket.

I inspect the fabric, where it's been cut by the blade. "What the hell?" I shout.

"Didn't you come to play?" he asks.

I go to move past him again, but he grabs my arm, spins me around, and backs me up against the brick wall. He's breathing hard and his breath reeks of coffee and oranges. He brings the ax high above his head, making like he's about to strike down.

I duck out of the way, pushing against him as I go. He lets out a laugh, as if my efforts are all a joke.

Straight ahead, a young boy appears on another screen. It's dark and he's in the middle of the woods, using a flashlight to find his way. "Craig?" the boy calls. "Paul?"

Craig and Paul are my brothers' names. The boy is supposed to be me.

A cabin comes into view. The Dark House. The sign is visible over the door. The boy knocks before going inside. There's a rocking chair with the Nightmare Elf doll.

"My name is Carson," the elf doll says, in his chipper voice. "Did you come to play?"

The boy begins to tremble.

I feel my stomach tie up in knots, remembering all those months I spent sleeping beneath the bed, praying that the Nightmare Elf would never visit my dreams.

The boy moves into a bedroom, tears sliding down his face. I want to tell him that it'll all be okay—that one day nothing will ever scare him again.

I turn away—it's too hard to watch—and follow the alleyway as it turns a corner. There's an open door at the rear of one of the buildings. I go inside, able to hear the rattle of the shopping cart again.

I close and lock the door behind me, trying to catch my breath, reminding myself that this is all for the movie. A dim overhead lightbulb hangs down from a ceiling with peeling paint. A concrete staircase is to my left. Another door faces me. I'm assuming the door leads underground. I pick the stairs and climb them, two at a time, until I reach the staircase platform.

There's a deep clink sound. The door lock? Before I can turn to look, the lightbulb goes out. The door I entered opens. I can hear footsteps coming up the stairs. I search the walls, desperate to find a door handle or light switch.

Footsteps continue. "Garth," the elf whispers. "Are you ready to join the fun?"

I find a knob and turn it, relieved when the door opens and I can see again. The hallway's lit up. I close the door behind me, noticing that it's an emergency exit, and that it doesn't have a lock.

There's a long red carpet that runs down the middle of the hall. The walls are covered in thick, purple paper. There are gold-framed mirrors, slanted ceilings, and crooked numbers on all the room doors. It's like being on the movie set of *Hotel 9*. I hurry down the hall until I reach the grand staircase—at least twenty steps high. It's framed in dark mahogany with balusters that look like evil serpents. Standing at the top, I look down at the lobby. More holograms. A group of kids in 1930s schoolboy garb—suit jackets, short pants, newsboy caps, and long kneesocks—play a game of Scrabble.

I look back over my shoulder, wondering where the elf is. The hallway remains empty.

Just then, a hologram of Sidney Scarcella enters the lobby. Wearing a butcher's apron over his bellboy uniform, he's carrying a pitcher of something dark. "More iced tea?" he asks the schoolboys.

They nod in creepy unison and he refills their glasses. I squint harder to see, accidentally brushing against the wall beside the banister. A picture falls—a family portrait of the Scarcellas. It tumbles down the flight of stairs. The glass inside the frame shatters.

"Garth, is that you?" One of the schoolboys stands. "Have you come to play?"

My forehead starts to sweat. I close my eyes a moment, noticing how unstable I feel on my feet.

"Garth, is that you?" the voice repeats. "Have you come to play?"

I scurry back down the hallway and try the knobs on a bunch of the room doors. Most of them are locked, but the one at the very end opens. I go inside and lock the door. It's dark, but I don't turn on the light; I don't want the elf to know where I am.

"You don't really think you can hide, do you?" a voice asks. "I have eyes everywhere."

I turn to look. It's Pudgy the Clown again. He clicks on his chain saw and starts running toward me.

I slip beneath the bed, flashing back to when I was seven. Quickly the chain saw quiets and the room goes dark again.

There's a knock at the door and a scratching sound on the wall. I hold my breath, wishing I were someplace else, feeling a dull ache in my belly. I have to piss. I'm going to throw up. Acid travels up my throat, choking me.

I roll out from under the bed, able to hear more scratching—fingernails on wood. A lighter striking over and over. And a key in the lock, turning. I move toward the window, able to see a shadow moving with me.

I try to open the window, wondering where I'd land if I jumped. But it's locked. I fumble with the latch, the sound of knives carving—blades scraping against each other—behind me.

"Ready to check out?" a voice asks from the darkness.

Finally, I get the lock unlatched. I open the window, just as my pants fill with heat as I lose it on the floor, pissing all over myself.

I dive out the window, headfirst, telling myself there must be a safety net.

It takes my brain a beat to realize that I've landed, that I'm no longer falling, that the smack sound is my body as it hits the pavement. I'm still alive. A numbing calmness. Moments later I hear it: the rattle of a shopping cart.

On my stomach, I try to inch forward.

The rattle grows louder.

I can see someone coming at me. A pair of elf boots covered in dirt. But I can't speak, can't scream. There's a flash of red.

He reaches down to feel for a pulse in my neck. Despite the gloves, he's wearing a bracelet. It dangles in front of my eyes: gold, chain-link, with the symbol for infinity. Frankie's bracelet. "You tried so hard to change," he says, "but you're still a scared seven-year-old boy."

There's the glare of an ax blade, and a deep moan as the ax is raised high.

IVY

AFTER THE OTHERS HAVE ALL DISPERSED, PARKER AND I decide to abandon Frankie's ride—for now, anyway—to try Taylor's phone at the front of the park. We stand beneath the TV monitor, where Justin Blake first spoke to us. I push the talk button and hold the receiver at varying angles, but it still isn't getting reception. "We can keep trying in different parts of the park," I say, hoping to sound optimistic. I look toward the top of the gate, wondering how many bones I'd break if I jumped from the very top, and what barbed wire feels like when it enters the skin.

"What are the odds of digging our way out of here?" I ask,

assuming the idea is nuts. But Parker looks at the gate for five full seconds and says it's worth a try.

We move over to it. I squat down and gaze upward, almost unable to see the wire at the very top—that's how far away it is.

Parker fetches a couple of plastic cups from a snack shack and hands me one. "Use it to shovel," he says, scooping up a mound of dirt.

I begin to dig, following the bars of the gate downward, into a hole. They seem to go on forever. I reposition, lying on my stomach, digging deeper into the ground.

"This isn't working," Parker says after about ten minutes. He tosses his broken cup and resumes digging, using his hands. The muscles in his forearms pulse. After about twenty more minutes, he steps inside his hole. He's almost up to his thighs, and still he hasn't reached the bottom of the gate. "It's like they knew we'd try to get out this way."

I sit at the edge of my ditch. "People are going to start to worry. Parents, I mean. Aside from Natalie and me, no one's called home yet—at least not that I know of, and it's been well over twenty-four hours now."

"Maybe we *should* venture underground," he says, nodding to the Train of Terror ride.

"No way." I shake my head. "Frankie and Shayla have both gone underground, and so far they've yet to resurface."

"We don't know that for a fact. Maybe they started underground but then followed a tunnel and came out someplace else. Let's face it, they could be anywhere—even beyond the gate." He nods to the forest.

I look out at the park. The actress on a nearby movie screen is running for her life. Naturally, she's in the woods, wearing heels instead of track shoes. She trips over a tree root and falls to the ground, letting out a sputtering noise that doesn't even sound human. She grapples forward on her elbows and knees.

I reach for my aromatherapy necklace, able to feel the girl's angst.

"What *is* that?" Parker asks, nodding to my necklace. He takes a seat beside me and our feet dangle inside my ditch.

"Cedarwood oil." I pull the cork out. "It helps induce tranquility and relaxation."

"Does it work?"

"You can be the judge."

"For real?" He goes to touch the bottle, checking for my reaction first.

I give him a silent okay and he moves in closer. His fingers graze my chest as he takes the bottle into his hand, sending tingles all over my skin.

Looking straight at me, he gives the bottle a tiny sniff. A

subtle grin sits on his lips, as if he knows his effect on me. "I feel better already," he says.

"Me too." I smile—my first one in what feels like days.

"Was it a present from someone that I should know about?"

"It was supposed to be my mom's."

"Supposed to be?"

I bite my lip, wishing that I could take the words back. "Maybe we should go look for more hotspots."

He nods and gets up, steps out from my ditch, and dusts the dirt from his palms. I can tell that he's frustrated with me. I'm frustrated with myself.

"There's a gamesmanship quality here," he says, before I can apologize. "Survive your worst nightmare, get to be in the movie, get to meet the mastermind. Knowing Blake's work, I'm pretty sure we're not getting out of here until we do that . . . face our nightmares, I mean. The main character always confronts the villain before the end. The showdown is not only expected, it's mandatory."

"And I signed up for this because . . . ?"

Parker looks at me again, his eyes swollen and serious. "I don't know; you won't tell me."

I swallow hard, hating myself for being so guarded. Yesterday, it probably wouldn't have mattered to me if he were upset by my secrecy. But today I'm upset too.

I don't want it to be like this.

"Let's get going." He extends his hand to help me up. I take it, feeling the warmth of his skin radiate over my face.

Parker notices and takes a step closer.

I try to glance away, but he forces me to look into his eyes by touching the side of my face. And making my heart pound. For just a moment I think that maybe he's going to kiss me. And, for the first time that I can remember, I actually want to be kissed. I want to believe that I can be just like every other girl, and not this person who's always waiting for the end.

Parker leans in a little closer and I stare at his lips—pale pink, shallow vee, slightly turned up at the corners. But before I can even feel his kiss, someone screams—a high-pitched shriek that severs the moment in two.

I turn to look. The girl on the screen—in the woods—is now running along a set of train tracks, while a dark-clothed someone follows behind her, keeping a steady pace.

"Let's go," Parker says. "We need to get this over with."

As we move toward the center of the park, a phone rings. I pull Taylor's cell phone out of my bag, but the ringing is coming from someplace else.

We follow the sound behind a row of Skee-Ball machines, startled to find a telephone booth.

"The emergency phone," I say, moving quickly to answer it. I push open the bifold door and grab the receiver. "Hello?"

"Who's this?" a male voice asks. "Wait, I think I might have the wrong number."

"No!" I insist. "Who is *this*? Who are you calling for?" I turn to look outward, spotting a first aid kit hanging on a nearby post.

"Is Max there?" the caller asks. "He left a message for me yesterday. Something about switching shifts. I'm just calling him back."

Parker comes and shares the receiver with me, his cheek grazing mine as we stand huddled in the booth.

"You have to listen to me," I say. "You have to help us. We're trapped inside an amusement park in the middle of the woods . . . someplace outside Stratten, Minnesota."

"Wait, so is Max *there*?" he asks.

Parker hangs up the phone.

"What are you doing?" I snap.

He presses the dial tone lever—again, and again, and again.

"What are you doing?" I repeat.

The dial tone never comes. Instead, the male voice is still there. He's laughing at us now. "Don't think you can get out of here without facing your nightmare. I need those scenes for the movie."

"News flash: we don't give a shit about the movie," Parker says.

"Well, you should, because surviving your ride is the only way out—the only way the gates will reopen."

"And what if we refuse?" I ask.

"Then consider yourself stuck inside these gates." The phone clicks. He hangs up.

Parker takes my hand and leads me away from the phone.

"Wait," I shout, stopping short. "Justin Blake can't do this. I mean, legally . . . he can't."

Parker's eyes lock on mine; he needs no words for me to know just what he's thinking: this isn't being run by Justin Blake. "Let's go," he says, taking my hand again.

We round a corner and come face-to-face with a giant water tank. "Sink or Swim," I say, reading the name on the sign.

"This is mine," he says, the color suddenly drained from his face. "I guess it's my turn."

PARKER

I CLIMB A LADDER THAT LEADS TO A PLATFORM overlooking a tank of water. The tank is a perfect square, about twelve feet long and wide. The water is murky brown, making me think of my essay. Not only did I lie about the eels, but I also changed the setting from the ocean to a pond. Another thing I lied about, not being able to swim. The fact is that getting swept up by a riptide and nearly drowning prompted me to become a great swimmer. A national, competitive swimmer.

A sign on the wall says ARE YOU READY TO SINK OR SWIM? According to the directions, I'll need to stay in the water for one full minute. A digital timer blinks the number sixty. The clock will begin counting down as soon as I enter the water. Then, once a minute's up, a bell will ring, indicating that I've succeeded.

The directions also state that should I want to get out at any point prior to the required minute, I can push one of the many emergency buzzers located at the water's edge. At that time, the "ride" will stop and a diver will assist me in getting out. I spot the emergency buzzers right away; they're positioned just above the water line. The idea of them should be reassuring, but I have no reason to trust anything about this weekend. Plus, where are the divers?

"You're going to be freezing," Ivy calls up to me. She's standing outside the ride, at the bottom of the ladder.

"I'll be fine," I say, trying to sound optimistic, even though I'm beyond uncertain. I pull off my T-shirt and take off my pants, socks, and sneakers, leaving only a pair of boxers. I turn to look down at Ivy and give her a little wink to be funny.

Gazing back at the water, I try to imagine that I'm on the other side of the camera—that this is a movie with me as the lead, or that I'm a contestant on a new reality game show. But neither scenario seems to stick, because this is real; I am here; I have to face this. My mental movie camera is temporarily broken.

I dive in. The water's cold, sending a shock wave through my body. Holding my breath, I plunge to the bottom. The tank is deeper than I expected—at least ten feet. Despite how much I don't want to be doing this, it's actually a relief to know that I lied—that no one can use a nightmare against me.

Once I reach the bottom, I kick off the cement surface and start to float upward. But then I feel it—something long and slick against my leg. I pop up, my head above the water now, and wait for what happens next.

Something sharp sinks into my calf. I struggle to swim to the side of the tank, unable to paddle fast enough. I reach down to feel the injured spot, just as something bites me again. My thigh this time.

I swim toward one of the emergency buzzers, my fingertips grazing the side of it, but I'm not close enough to push it down.

I fall beneath the surface of the water. My mouth fills up with muck. I resurface and spit it out. My skin's torn. My leg's bleeding. Spotlights shine over the water, enabling me to see the color red mix with brown.

I go for the buzzer again—this time able to reach it. I smack it, but it makes no noise. I punch it, slap it, beat it with my fist. Still nothing.

"Parker!" Ivy shouts. She says something else, but I can't quite hear her.

That's when I see them: long and black, cresting the water, coming at me.

Eels.

They're attracted by my blood. I duck my head and plunge, leaving the blood in my wake, hoping it'll be enough to satisfy them for now. But I can feel them swimming between my legs and biting at my feet. Teeth sink into the arch of my foot and I let out a howl beneath the water. My mouth fills up once more.

I kick the eel away, swim to the surface, and smack another buzzer. Still no sound. No divers, either. I look up at the digital timer. Twenty-two more seconds.

"Parker!" Ivy calls out.

"Stay down there," I tell her.

Fifteen seconds left.

Eels swarm at my wounds. I can feel the slickness against my skin. My hands bracing the sides of the tank, I try to lift myself out, but I'm bitten on the back of my knee. The pain radiates down my calf and I fall back in, slipping beneath the surface once more. Treading water, I try to swat the eels away. There have to be at least twenty of them in here.

"I'm coming up there," Ivy says.

"No!" I shout. I try to stay above the surface, but I keep sinking deeper, my head spinning with questions. Will I ever make it out of here? How can this possibly be happening?

An eel swims between my legs. I grab it—it's at least four inches thick—and try to lift it out, but it's too heavy, too strong.

It lunges for me, nipping at my side. An instant surge of blood.

I scream beneath the surface. Water fills my mouth. Something gets caught in the back of my throat, creating a choking sensation. I reach in to yank it out—a leaf. A piece of it lingers, making me want to gag.

Still, I fight to swim upward, feeling a tug at my thigh—teeth ripping through the flesh.

My hands hit something hard. I'm at the bottom of the tank, or maybe it's the side. I'm turned around, disoriented, having lost my sense of direction.

I somersault in the water, able to find my feet against a hard surface. I kick off with all my might, following the direction of my air bubbles as I struggle to reach the top.

Not quite there, I see something moving out of the corner of my eye.

Holy freaking shit.

It's a steel cover—just like in my bogus nightmare essay.

The cover expands the width of the water's surface, moving steadily across the top, closing in the tank.

Finally, I crest the water. I reach up to grab the ledge of the tank, hearing myself gasp. My lungs are aching. I can't seem to get enough air. The steel cover is only a few feet away, getting closer with each breath.

"Parker!" Ivy shouts.

The digital clock has timed out. Zero seconds left. I lose my grip on the ledge and fall beneath the surface once more.

The cover is within arm's reach. I swim upward and grab the edge of it, trying to hold it in place. My biceps ache. My forearms throb. The cover continues to push forward, closing me in, trapping me inside.

I swim to the side of the tank again. With one hand on the platform, I'm able to hoist myself up, gaining leverage with my elbow, and then with my knee. The cover grazes my foot as it seals over the surface of the water.

Up on the platform, I collapse into a mass of blood and throbbing muscles. The leaf's still stuck in my throat. I force it out, sticking my fingers into my mouth, hacking up a piece of a stem.

Ivy joins me on the platform. She rubs my back and tells me that it's all over. But it isn't. Far from it. Because now it's her turn.

NATALIE

GARTH'S RIGHT. WE'RE HERE FOR A REASON. AND IT'D
be crazy to walk away from an opportunity this monumental.
And so after he takes off to find his nightmare, I head off to find
mine, despite what Harris says.

"You have to understand how much this means to me," I tell
him. "Justin Blake has really been there for me."

"And I haven't?"

"Of course, but this is different. He was there for me in ways
that you couldn't be."

"Well, then maybe you don't need me at all."

"That's not what I mean, Harris."

"Don't do this, Nat. If you don't listen to me ever again, listen to this: get out of there. If you don't, you just might join me . . . on this side."

I pull out more hair—from my eyelashes this time—wishing that his words didn't burrow so deeply into my heart.

I circle the park for a third time, still searching for my ride. We passed by it earlier, but I wasn't ready to go in at that point, especially with Harris's barking.

"Are you a little lost?" a voice asks, just behind me.

I turn to look. There's a movie screen there. On it is Little Sally Jacobs from *Night Terrors*, wearing a pair of pink sunglasses to hide her skeleton-key-punctured eyes. It's mid-scene and she's asking Mrs. Baker, a new neighbor, if she'd like to come inside the house for a glass of lemonade.

"You can meet my parents," Sally says, sweetening the deal. "Mama just made the lemonade this morning. She should also have some cookies coming out of the oven right about now."

This part of the movie—when the woman follows Sally inside—kept me awake for hours, because I knew just what would happen. And I was right. Mrs. Baker never came out.

I watch the scene for several moments before gazing around at the other movie screens scattered about the park: all of Justin Blake's films at various points in the story—some in the middle

(Lizzy Greer chasing a streetwalker with an ax), others at the climax (Eureka trying to escape Pudgy the Clown, in some overhead ductwork). It appears that *Forest of Fright* just started, and the end credits are rolling on *Halls of Horror*, toward the center of the park.

At last, I spot my nightmare ride; it's called Mirrors of Mayhem, and it's basically a fun-house maze of mirrors.

It's dark as I approach. There's a blacked out door at the front. I climb the steps to enter, but it's locked.

"What the hell?" I shout, jiggling the handle and pushing my weight against the door panel.

Still, it won't open—even after ten minutes.

I scurry down the steps and circle the ride, searching for another way in, wondering if maybe there's some trick.

Finally, the "ride" lights up, as if by magic. Music pours out of it—a mix of organ and harmonica.

As I climb the steps again, the music grows louder, making it nearly impossible to hear Harris. Still, I know his voice is there. I can hear it, struggling over the music—like someone fighting to keep above water, only to end up drowned out by the waves.

I enter the walls of glass and the floor begins to rotate. I take careful steps, trying to avoid eye contact with my reflection by keeping my focus down. But it's absolutely no use. My reflection is everywhere—in front of me, beside me, cut in half, multiplied by five, as part of a giant mosaic of shapes. My Scissorhands hair, my crooked nose, my pudgy lips.

Arms too long.

Hips too wide.

Swollen skin from picking, plucking, pulling, pinching.

My face flashes red. In one mirror, I'm short and bulging, with stocky legs, a gigantic stomach, and a tiny head. In another mirror, I'm all stretched out and my face looks even longer than it is.

I try to turn around, to get out, but I'm already lost in the maze of my reflection. I shut my eyes and extend my hands to feel my way around so I don't have to look. But I manage to bump into the glass anyway—my cheek brushes against a corner of a glass panel. I open my eyes, catching sight of the brown mole on my upper lip. It looks bigger than I remember. Puffier than ever before. Is this another distortion mirror?

I turn away, smacking into another glass pane—my nose this time. My sunglasses fall off. Blood trickles from a nostril, over my lips, and drips off my chin, landing on yet another image of me—so much worse without the glasses, in the light. I'm standing on a mirror. Another droplet of blood hits the reflection below my feet.

There's more red—a flash of it reflected in the mirror. Someone's moving behind me, behind another section of glass. And yet I don't see a face. The image is too fast and fleeting. The redness whirls and ripples, as if the person's wearing a cape.

I turn, following the figure with my eyes. Finally, the image stops. I see a slice of red, perfectly still. I wait, breathing hard. My breath steams up the mirror, making an oblong stain against the glass, covering my forehead.

At last, I see who it is. The Nightmare Elf—most likely the same man who appeared on the TV screen when we entered the park, wearing a mask that has pointed ears, chubby cheeks, and curly blond hair. The mask is stuck in a perpetual grin; the forehead of it is shiny, as if it's somehow sweating too.

"You know why the elf is here, don't you?" Harris asks, ripping a hole in my heart.

Why is he so hell-bent on hurting me, on ruining this experience?

"What experience?" he asks. *"Is this what you call a fun time?"*

I hold my bloody nose. Where did my sunglasses go? I don't see them anywhere now. I keep looking for an exit. But, just one step away, I bump into a wall. The elf starts laughing. His head tilts back, jittering slightly, and he holds on to his belly. I sniff up the blood and extend my arms again, moving out from behind a pane of glass, trying my best not to cry.

The Nightmare Elf moves too. One moment I think he's in front of me, the next he's behind me again.

Then at my right.

And over to my left.

The reflections are too overwhelming. I'm standing in an alcove of a thousand mini-reflections of me. They make a checker-board pattern, boxing me in, stealing my breath.

There's not much air. My chest feels tight.

A swirl of red dances around me and then does a cartwheel behind my back.

I try to get out of this alcove. I move to the side and then inch into what I think is another area, but it looks exactly the same; the checkerboard pattern surrounds me on all sides. I look up. There are mirrors there, too. And still more mirrors as I turn around—as if the thousand have somehow quadrupled.

Finally, the music stops. There's a rushing sensation inside my veins. I don't see the elf anywhere. There's just my reflection every way I turn.

I move out from behind a glass panel, but I'm blocked. There are mirrored walls all around me now, as if someone's locked me in.

I run my fingers up and down the panes, my breath fogging up the glass, wondering if there might be an empty space I'm not seeing. The Nightmare Elf giggles, but still I can't see him. I'm feeling more trapped by the moment. My throat constricts. I can't get enough air.

"I'm really sorry, Nat," Harris says. *"I wish you would've listened."*

I turn around and around as the floor beneath me continues to rotate. My head is dizzy. I stumble over my feet.

Suddenly, a wall goes black. I reach out to touch it just as a light clicks on inside it. The Nightmare Elf is there, on the other side. He waves at me with his glove-covered hand.

"He's come to watch you suffer," Harris says. *"The elf always appears at the time of death. After he steals your nightmare and uses it against you, he comes around to watch his dirty work play out."*

"Stop!" I scream. Blood spouts out of my mouth, from my nose, spraying the glass. I cover my fists with the sleeves of my jacket and then pound against one of the walls.

Nothing happens.

I pound harder, kicking the glass with my boot. The mirror breaks. But there's another mirror in its place, just behind it.

The elf laughs harder.

Harris begins to pray: *"Hail Mary, full of grace . . ."*

My heart beats faster. My pulse races harder. I start throwing my body against the glass walls, beating the panes with my fists, kicking as hard as I can.

Glass shatters, cutting into my skin, making everything red. Thousands of years of bad luck. I look up, just as a giant shard of glass slices downward.

Ivy

PARKER IS REALLY BLEEDING. LYING ON HIS BACK, he's breathing hard, shivering from either fear or pure coldness. There's a bite mark on his side, two in his left thigh, and a few more on his calves and feet.

I take off my sweatshirt and blanket it over his chest, along with Natalie's scarf. "I'll be right back." I run down the stairs, round the corner by the phone booth, and see the first aid kit in the distance, hanging on a post.

Despite the blinking lights, the park feels vacant, especially without Parker by my side. It's quiet, as if someone's muted the volume, shut off the music, and pulled the plug on all the movie projectors.

The air is warm and thick as I move toward the post. Just a few yards away from it now, I hear something: the sound of footsteps, the crunching of gravel.

I stop and look around. Nothing.

I turn back to head for the first aid kit. There's a scuffing sound behind me again. "Who's there?" I call out.

No one answers.

An owl hoots in the distance as I grab the first aid kit. It's a metal box with sharp corners. I position it in my hands with a corner pointed outward, ready to use it as a weapon if need be.

I hurry back to the Sink or Swim ride and scurry up the stairs, two at a time, tripping on the tread at the very top. I kneel down by Parker's side, trying to catch my breath. "We'll get through this," I tell him.

I doubt that he believes me. I hardly believe myself.

Parker turns away from the tank, trying not to show too much emotion, even though his wounds are raw and weeping.

I pop open the emergency kit. Inside is a picture of first aid supplies. Otherwise, the box is empty. My heart clenches. My face flashes hot. I want to scream at the top of my lungs, but I hold in my emotion too.

I reach into my bag, grateful to have brought along a few tea bags. Since his skin is already wet, I'm able to apply them directly to the wounds, placing one on the bite on his thigh, another on the bite on his waist, and then my last one on his ankle.

"What are you doing?" he asks.

"Tea contains tannins," I explain, pressing the tea bag against his ankle. His calf muscle flexes in response. "And tannins help clot blood. They also act as a natural astringent, which means there may be less chance of an infection." The golden hair that covers his legs appears slightly curly from the dampness. I wonder how it would feel against my skin. I swallow hard, trying to stay focused, noticing a large bite mark at the back of his knee. I flip one of the tea bags over to the fresh side and press it firmly against the spot.

Parker flinches from the pressure. "Lucky for me that you just happen to carry tea bags around in your purse."

"I think I may've mentioned that tea is sort of my vice."

"Sounds more like a serious problem. Should I be staging an intervention?"

"Surprisingly chipper for escaping a tank full of hungry eels, aren't we?"

"Are you kidding? If I knew it'd mean getting this kind of treatment, I'd have been eel bait hours ago."

I apply a bit more pressure to the wound. "You're a really good clotter, you know that?"

"Should I feel special, or do you say that to all your flesh-eating-eel victims?"

"You should feel special," I say, surprised by his persistence in flirting, especially all things considered.

I spend the next several minutes treating his wounds before I can no longer hold in the question: "What's happening here?"

Parker sits up and reaches for his clothes, his whole demeanor shifted—from somewhat optimistic to totally dismal.

"I mean, what would've happened if you hadn't gotten out of there?" I continue.

He pulls his T-shirt on over his head—over his smooth, tan chest. "I don't even want to think about it."

"Okay, but we have to think about it. You could've died in there."

"Bottom line: you shouldn't go on your nightmare ride."

"Is that why we haven't seen the others?" I ask. "Because they didn't make it out of their own nightmare rides?"

"Unless maybe they escaped?"

"And maybe Blake has nothing to do with this contest."

"There's no maybe there. I suspected that something was off as soon as we stepped inside those gates. When Justin Blake appeared on the screen, I could tell that it wasn't real—just a bunch of sound bites edited together. The real Justin Blake has too much to lose."

"So where do we go from here?"

"Tell me about your nightmare," he says.

"I want to."

"But what? My sexy bloodstained physique intimidates you?" He tries to stand, but the bites on his legs make him wince. He grabs his pants anyway, my cue to turn around.

A second later, I hear something drop to the ground. His boxer shorts, sopping wet. I can see them out of the corner of my eye. The sound is followed by the swish of jeans as he yanks them on.

"It's safe," he says.

Still sitting, I swivel around to face him. His hair is damp and tousled. The cotton of his T-shirt sticks to the muscles of his chest. And his jeans hug his upper thighs.

"Well?" he asks.

At first I think he's asking me how he looks. But then he sits back down, takes my hands, and tells me that I can trust him. "If it'll make you feel any better, I can tell you about a real nightmare that I once had."

"No more stories about eels?"

"No eels," he says. "When I was seven, I wandered off in a department store and couldn't find my mom afterward. I ended up in the boys' bathroom, crying in one of the stalls. Finally, a worker found me and brought me up to the service desk, where my mom was crying too. Anyway, for months afterward, I had nightmares about getting left behind in various places—on a road trip, at the grocery store, in the shopping mall—no matter how many times I made my mother promise that she'd never lose me again."

"Oh my gosh, that's so sad."

"Now, your turn. And keep in mind that nothing you say about your nightmare is going to freak me out."

"Don't be too sure about that."

"You're a lot stronger than you know," he says. "I mean, you made it here, didn't you? You entered this contest, you got on a plane."

"My parents were murdered," I tell him. "Six years ago. In their bedroom. I was home when it happened."

Parker studies my face, perhaps waiting for me to tell him it's only a joke. "Who did it?" he asks, finally.

"They never caught the guy, but they know he's a serial killer. He murdered a few other people before my parents, always playing music at the scene of the crime."

His faces furrows. *"Music?"*

"Scores from various horror movies—*Psycho, The Shining, Halloween*. He was a big fan of the genre. His killings—the style in which he did them—were copycat murders from the films. For my parents, it was the bedroom scene from *Haunt Me*."

Parker grimaces, perhaps picturing the scene. "I know that film."

"That's one of the biggest reasons I came on this trip—to meet people who love horror, that is. To learn from them. To see horror as a source of entertainment, rather than the bane of my existence."

"And how's that working out for you so far?"

"I'm cured, can't you tell?" I look at the tank. "Just when you thought it was safe to go back into the water."

"*Jaws II*, have you seen it?" He smirks.

"What do *you* think?" I smirk back. "Anyway, the guy who killed my parents, we made eye contact. I saw his face. And after everything was over, I had to change my identity and move in with a foster family. Natalie was right . . . I don't like being filmed. I don't want to risk that he might one day recognize me."

Parker looks down at our hands, still gripped together, and for five horrible seconds, I think he's going to let go. But instead he squeezes my hands tighter.

"His eyes have haunted my nightmares ever since that night," I continue. "I don't want to relive what happened."

Parker looks deeply into my eyes. Part of me wants so badly to glance away. But I don't, even as he breaks the clasp of my hands, and slides his fingers along my face, setting fire to my skin. "Do you want to hear what a nightmare would be for me *now*?"

"What a nightmare *would be*?"

"Going home after this weekend and never seeing you again."

"Seriously?" I ask, waiting for the punch line.

His eyes remain steady and somber. "Promise me that won't happen, okay?"

"I promise." I nod.

He runs his thumb over my lips, awakening every last nerve inside my body. My head feels spinny as his lips press against mine, feeding the aching deep inside me. His kiss is soft and sweet and salty inside my mouth. My hands move over the muscles in his forearms. Heat spills across my thighs and over my hips. I want so badly to crawl up right inside of him—into the part that knows no fear.

"Ivy," he whispers, once the kiss ends. He's slightly out of breath.

Meanwhile, my entire body quivers.

"You're right," he says. "We're going to get through this."

"Maybe we should wait the night out," I suggest. "It'll be sunrise before we know it."

"Except I don't think sunrise is going to get us out of here."

"So, then what do you suggest?"

"Keep looking for hotspots, keep trying to find a way out.

And, in the meantime, try to focus on what happens after we get out of here." His pale blue eyes stare into mine, and once again I don't look away.

I don't ever want to look away again.

"There's so much about you that I want to know," he continues.

"Really?" I ask, almost unable to imagine the idea of anyone wanting to know me: this person who's seen too much, this girl who might still be in danger.

"Will you let me?"

I nod, unable to hold myself back. And so I lean in to kiss him again, almost forgetting where we are, and what we're doing here.

"I'm not going to let you go," he says, once the kiss breaks. "After the weekend, I mean. I think it's fairly safe to say that you're stuck with me. If that's okay, that is."

"Definitely okay."

Parker reaches out to take my hand, and together we move down the stairs, beyond his ride, past a Forest of Fright Tilt-A-Whirl and a ride called Nightmare Alley. We round a corner.

And that's when I see it.

Again.

We passed by it when we first entered the park, only I wasn't quite ready to look at it then—not that I'm feeling particularly ready now.

My nightmare ride.

A small yellow house with a white picket fence.

"Ivy?" Parker asks.

I look toward the door, silently acknowledging the fact that I've been dreaming about my parents' killer for the past six years, and so when you stop to think about it—"I've given myself six years to prepare for this moment," I say.

"Don't do this." He grips my hands, as if trying to squeeze some sense into me.

I pull away, feeling a chill. "I have to," I whisper.

Keeping a firm grip on my mother's necklace, I begin up the walkway, anticipating what awaits me inside. Is it possible that I'll learn something about my parents? Or maybe about that night?

Parker calls out to me, telling me to shout if I need anything, promising to come looking for me if I'm not out in ten minutes.

The door swings shut behind me. A foyer light brightens the entryway. The layout of the house is different from my childhood home. The stairwell is on the left rather than the right, there's no hallway closet, and the walls are painted blue rather than covered with rose-colored wallpaper.

There are framed photographs on the wall. They're obviously different from the ones that had lined the stairwell of the real 3 Mulberry Road, but still the idea is the same. They're photographs of me, available online: a picture taken by the local paper at my eighth-grade graduation and a photo of me on a recent school camping trip.

My bedroom is to the right at the top of the stairs. My parents' room is on the left. Their door is closed. My head feels woozy. I reach out, my fingers trembling, to try the knob, but it's locked.

I head into my room and flick on the light, but it doesn't work. Only the dim hallway light seeps into the space. Exactly like that night.

I breathe in and out, trying to stay present in the moment, as Dr. Donna advises.

My room looks right: the pink paisley bed linens, the faux-fur beanbag chair, the soccer banners and Katrina Rowe posters.

I sit on the bed, flashing back to that night—awakening from a thrashing sound across the hall, then hearing a gasp, a sputter, and an agonizing moan. Those noises were followed by a stifling silence, interrupted by a voice: "And now it's your turn."

I pull Taylor's cell phone from my bag, remembering the phone receiver that I had that night—a cordless extension from the kitchen.

I dial 9-1-1, just as I did that night, knowing the phone won't work. And I'm right. It doesn't. Instead, a thrashing sound tears through the silence.

It's happening again. I'm twelve years old. I pinch the skin on my knee.

Music begins to play—a blend of violin and viola. I clench the bed covers, still trying to get the phone to work. But then it slips from my grip and falls to the floor. Bile fills my mouth. I swallow it down and take a deep breath, reminding myself:

I'm no longer twelve years old.

Parker is right outside.

The door to my parents' bedroom opens. The music grows louder. A man's there, dressed as the Nightmare Elf in a red suit and hat. He's wearing a mask. The elf's grin is frozen on his face.

"Good evening, Princess," he whispers. "It's *very* nice to meet you." The words send shivers all over my skin.

Unlike six years ago, there are no sirens in the background, no response to any 9-1-1 calls.

I clench my teeth, feeling a flood of emotion overcome me: fear, anger, regret. There have been six years of emotions before I got to this moment.

Before I got to this moment, I took self defense classes every Saturday morning. And slept with a kitchen knife under my pillow. And walked to and from school with a can of bug spray in my pocket. I imagined this very scene at least a thousand times, and yet it still feels like a dream.

A nightmare.

I mean, it can't possibly be happening, can it?

He turns the knife in his gloved hand. It's a six-inch,

spring-spike, double-action blade, like the one that killed my parents.

I reposition myself on the bed, unfolding my legs from beneath me, and pressing my back up against the wall.

He moves closer. Standing over me, he pokes the tip of the blade into my neck. "You knew I'd come back, didn't you?"

The blade pokes deeper with the motion of my throat as I swallow. He cocks his head, studying my face.

I press my back harder against the wall. My legs bent in front of me, I kick outward. My heel plunges into his gut.

He stumbles back, but comes at me with the knife again, holding it at my jugular. "A quick incision is all it'll take. Just tell me when you're ready." He glides the blade across my skin. "Be a good girl now," he sings.

Just then, something pelts against the window. He turns to look and I grab his arm. I bring it up to my mouth and bite down through his sleeve, into his flesh. He lets out a wail. The knife drops from his grip.

I reach for it, but he snatches it away before I can get it. I move quickly, scrambling to the foot of the bed, struggling to get to the door. But he grabs my leg, holding me in place, slashing my ankle. At least four inches.

I tumble off the bed. My cheek smacks against the hardwood

floor. Lying on my belly, I search the room for something—*anything*—to protect myself with. I spot a metal ruler on the desk. I begin toward it, grappling forward on my elbows, but he steps on my hand, freezing me in place. The heel of his boot grinds down into my fingers, cracking the knuckles, burning the skin.

Parker shouts my name from outside.

"Your friend won't be able to get in," he says, standing over me now. "The doors are locked. The windows have bars. It's just you and me now, Princess."

I roll over to face him and he kneels down, pinning me against the floor with the knife. I swallow, feeling the point of the blade cut into my skin, just above my collarbone. A trickle of blood runs across my chest, soaking into his glove.

Breathing hard, I look toward his waist, wondering if I could kick him again—if it'd make enough of an impact from this angle, or if exerting myself would only push the knife in deeper.

"Please," I whisper, able to hear the desperation in my voice, trying to think of something clever to say.

A giant crash sounds. I feel it in my bones, but it's in the room. The window broke. He straightens up to look.

I kick him—*hard*—plunging the heel of my shoe into his groin. He doubles over, letting out a grunt. The knife flies from his grip. I crawl across the floor and manage to grab it.

I get back on my feet, holding the knife out toward him, gripped in both hands.

He straightens up again. "Be careful with that, Princess." Standing just a couple of feet away, he approaches me slowly, his arms extended.

"Don't!" I shout.

He lunges at me. His hands wrap around mine as he tries to wriggle the knife from my grip.

"No!" I thrust the knife forward, plunging it deep into his side, in the space between his ribs.

He lets out a gasp. His eyes slam shut. He stumbles back.

I turn away and bolt out of the bedroom, closing the door behind me.

The door to my parents' room is open a crack. I push it wider, able to picture their room that night: the blood on the wall, over the bed, soaking the sheets, filling the cracks of the hardwood floors.

I cover my mouth, shaking my head.

"Ivy!" Parker shouts from outside, snapping me back to the moment.

I tear down the stairs, missing at least three of the treads toward the bottom. I propel forward, headfirst, somehow catching myself. I go to open the front door, but it's the kind that locks automatically. The lock doesn't turn. It seems to be stuck. I can't quite get my fingers to work right.

I can hear him upstairs. The clunking of footsteps, the thwacking of wood against the wall as he flings the door open.

Finally, I get the lock unstuck and flee outside, slamming the door behind me.

PARKER

EXT. IVY'S NIGHTMARE RIDE—NIGHT

A small yellow house with a picket fence and
bars on the windows. I'm just about to throw
another brick at the window glass, when I
hear something at the door—the sound of a
LOCK TURNING. The knob RATTLES.

Ivy comes flying out of the house, tears
streaming down her face. Blood stains the

bottom of her pants. Her leg's bleeding. A
sideways slit.

I drop my mental camera and pull off my T-shirt. I tear a piece
of fabric and wrap it around her ankle as a bandage.

"My bag," she says, checking her shoulder. There's nothing
there. "I left it. I lost Taylor's phone." She looks back at the
house, just as a TV screen lights up behind us. The costumed
Nightmare Elf appears on the screen—most likely the same guy
from the welcome video, the one dressed in the elf costume.

"Greetings, Dark House Dreamers," he says. "Congratulations on facing your nightmares . . . *and surviving them.*" He
releases a maniacal laugh. "Now, how would you like to see a
rough cut of the film? I do hope you'll enjoy it."

Numbers flash across the screen, from ten down to one. The
screen goes black, and then gets punctured by the image of head-
lights. *Welcome to the Dark House* appears in red crayon. The
movie starts: there's a car driving down a gravel road. Trees and
brush surround the car on both sides.

The next thing I know, the name Ivy Jensen appears in the
credits. It's followed by my name and then Natalie Sorrento. The
car continues, angled toward us on the screen, before finally coming to a stop.

"It's us," I say, able to see now that the car is actually a hearse.

Ivy gets out and stares up at the WELCOME TO THE DARK HOUSE sign. More credits continue to roll: Frankie Rice, Shayla Belmont, Garth Vader, Taylor Monroe.

The film looks like it was professionally done, like whoever did it knows how to work a camera, but still, it's not Justin Blake's work—not the lighting, nor the audio, and certainly not the camera angles.

My bite marks throbbing, I keep one leg slightly elevated as I hold Ivy close, watching as our night at the Dark House unfolds. I've seen most of the content before, but some of it is new: a blond girl—who I assume to be Taylor—applying a thick coat of lipstick; Garth uncovering a splotch of blood in Taylor's closet; and Ivy watching me sleep—the same way I had watched her sleep. There's also a close-up of Garth and Shayla kissing, and of Frankie in the hallway, bummed that he's not the one she's with. We fade out on a back shot of Taylor as she flees the Dark House, into the woods.

Ivy huddles closer as we watch the scene where we enter the amusement park through the tall iron gate, as Shayla and Garth start cheering, and as we all stand beneath that first TV screen, where Justin Blake supposedly spoke to us. The shot dissolves on the tense expression on Ivy's face—the same one that's on her face now.

It's clear that the movie has been at least partially edited. I can tell by all the cutaways—each of us on the Nightmare Elf's Train of Terror ride, all experiencing different things.

Finally, we get to Frankie's ride. Anxiety bubbles in my stomach as Frankie enters the shed at the back of the graveyard. After a phone call fiasco, he finds a trapdoor and descends a ladder, going down to an underground graveyard.

He moves toward the back row, where there's a giant hole in the ground. The camera zooms in on a gravestone. Frankie's name is engraved in the polished marble. Beneath it are dates—what I'm assuming is Frankie's date of birth, plus today's date.

A moment later, there's a ringing sound. It takes me a beat to realize that it's coming from the movie. A phone's been buried; the ringing is coming from inside the hole.

Frankie climbs down into it, desperate to answer the call. He starts digging deeper, slinging the dirt with a shovel, creating a pile by his feet.

"Where's the phone?" Ivy whispers.

A coffin appears. A skeleton. A watch. The camera refocuses, angling on Frankie as dirt comes down on him from above.

Eventually burying him alive.

His screams have blades; they cut a hole in my gut. "Holy shit," I whisper, over and over again, almost unable to take it anymore.

Ivy's face is full of tears. She holds her aromatherapy necklace up to her lips.

The scene fades to black, and then we cut to Shayla. She found Frankie's grave. But then a noise startles her and she moves down a tunnel—what appears to be a mine—where she finds a body hanging in a closet; I can't tell if it's real. The camera angles on the Nightmare Elf. He approaches her from behind and lifts her up by the neck. Her feet flutter in the air as she struggles to break free. The last thing we hear from Shayla is the sound of her body as it drops to the ground.

The scene switches again. We're with Garth in his nightmare ride now. There are holograms and movie clips. Garth moves down a long, dark alleyway, dodging a dangerous encounter with the Nightmare Elf, trying to seek refuge in Hotel 9. The ride ends with Garth jumping out of a window. There's a close-up of him landing facedown against the pavement below. The Nightmare Elf appears again. The scene cuts just as his ax is raised high.

Ivy lets out a gasp that rivals mine. She's crying uncontrollably, her chest heaving in and out.

The scene changes once more. It's Natalie's turn now, but the film quality has changed. None of it looks edited. It's more like footage tacked on from surveillance video. Natalie's trapped inside a house of mirrors, pounding against the glass. The mirrors eventually shatter and cut into her skin. Blood sprays everywhere. Natalie's screams are hoarse and desperate, I can feel them in my chest. But then I don't hear them at all. The silence is far worse than her screaming.

There's more footage too—of the disappointment in Ivy's eyes when Eureka Dash's scream interrupted our moment by the gate, of me entering the eel tank, and of Ivy and me kissing.

Finally, the closing credits roll. The screen goes black again. Then Ivy and I appear live, on the screen. The camera's on us.

"You've made it," the elf says. "The lone survivors, worthy of seeing the rough-cut. And now, as promised, I have a sneaking suspicion that you might be ready to leave the park. Am I right?"

"Where is he?" Ivy whispers, looking over both shoulders. She repeats the question, over and over, faster and faster.

"The entrance gates will reopen at the count of three," the voice says. "You will then have exactly ten seconds to get out. If you don't make it, don't despair; consider yourself a lead part in the sequel." He snickers. "Now, are we ready?"

I look in the direction of the entrance gates.

"One, two . . ."

Before he can get to three, Ivy and I make a beeline to escape. Keeping pace behind her, I hobble past a slew of games. Past the merry-go-round, the strong-arm challenge, and the Nightmare Elf's Train of Terror.

I hear the entrance gates unlatch. The doors begin to creak open. The bites on my legs are throbbing. The one on the back of my knee burns with each step.

Just shy of getting to the gate, Ivy's necklace falls to the ground, but she doesn't notice. I stop to pick it up. The bite at my side stings as I bend forward. There's a pulling-stretching sensation, and I let out a grunt. The pendant slips free of the chain. Sweat drips, stinging my eyes.

"Parker!" Ivy shouts.

I scurry to pick up the pendant, blood drooling down my leg and from my waist. And then I start moving toward the gates again, limping as fast as I can.

I trip and fall to my knees.

The gates have started to close.

Ivy's already free, already on the other side. "Hurry!" she shouts. She struggles to hold the gates open, but the doors are far too heavy. I see her getting dragged, using all her weight against the steel bars.

I get up and hobble forward, feeling my eyes fill with tears. I'm not moving quickly enough. There's no way I'm going to get there in time.

The gates lock shut just short of my getting there.

"No!" Ivy screams. Her voice echoes inside my head, bouncing off the bones of my skull.

I'm locked inside with no way out.

"We'll get you out of there," she says, grabbing my hands through the bars.

Meanwhile, I'm crying too hard for words, no longer able to hold in my emotion. The necklace falls from my grip.

"One of those underground tunnels has to lead outside," she says. "Or maybe we can try digging again."

"Just go," I say, shaking my head, knowing that she can't stay.

"I'm not going anywhere. Not without you."

"You need to get help," I tell her. "Then come back for me."

"I won't leave you," she insists, crying even harder now.

"You have to," I say, looking away, not wanting her to see what a mess I am.

Eventually, she picks up the necklace and places it back in my hand. "Hold on to this," she says. "Until I come back, okay?"

"Just promise me you'll come back."

She kisses me through the bars. Her lips are warm, her breath is hot. I can feel her tears on my skin, can already feel her absence in my heart.

"More than promise," she says, before kissing me one final time. After that, she turns on her heel, and escapes into the night.

Autumn

IVY

I PULL DOWN THE GRAVEL ROAD THAT LEADS TO THE amusement park. My car is compact and I'm able to pull up in front of the gate.

It appears that I'm alone. The sign welcoming me to the amusement park still hangs above the entrance, only it's no longer illuminated, and the words are slightly crooked.

I get out of the car. It's midday and the air is chilled, especially with the tree boughs shrouding the area. I go up to the gate, past the police tape that tells me not to. It's amazing how different things look in the daylight, no longer sparkly and alluring, but stark, drab, and haunted. I reach out through the bars, picturing Parker on the other side, the pleading look in his eyes, the tears running down his face.

I hate myself for leaving him here.

After I escaped and made it to the street, and flagged down help, called the police, and showed them where to look, it was two hours later and Parker couldn't be found.

The others couldn't either. Not even Frankie. When investigators went to dig him up, all they found was an empty hole.

The investigation turned cold quickly. The FBI believes whoever is responsible is smart, rich, and demented. The rest remains a mystery—a string of false leads and dead ends.

I look back at the welcome sign, thinking how excited everyone was by it. The statue of Eureka is still there too, only it's been blasted with a paintball gun. There are splotches of orange and green over her smiling wooden face.

This gated entrance area has been littered, too: soda cans, beer bottles, and snack packages strewn all over the ground— new and old Blake fans, desperate to get a taste of the "fun."

The sound of creaking metal startles me. The Nightmare Elf's Train of Terror must have a few loose hinges. The tarp on the snack shack rustles in the breeze. A set of wind chimes jangles.

A gust sweeps over my shoulders, blowing back my hair. I

turn to get an extra scarf. But then I come to a sudden halt. I blink a couple of times, trying to make sense of what I see.

The Nightmare Elf doll. It's perched on the roof of my car. The same doll that we found in Tommy's nightmare chamber, with the missing eye and the dirty clothes.

My chest tightens. My mind begins to race. I look around— in the trees, down the road, beneath my car, in the park. But I don't see a single soul.

The gate creaks, making me jump. I turn to look. It's open a crack—just enough for me to slip through.

Music begins to play. The musical score to *Haunt Me*. The layering of violins, that haunting viola, the strum of the cello. It's coming from behind the merry-go-round, from my nightmare ride; I'm sure of it.

He's been waiting for me to come back.

I grab my keys, positioning the sharpest one—ironically, a skeleton key, just like Little Sally Jacobs's—between my index and middle fingers, ready to fight. And then I move through the gate and across the park, toward the merry-go-round, pausing at one of the horses. Its eyes are slanted and blue, reminding me of Parker's. Its golden mane is the same color as Parker's hair, too. It's crying bloody tears.

The merry-go-round music starts up, but it's so slow and tired that eventually it stops playing altogether.

But still the musical score to *Haunt Me* lingers—a pulsing beat that pelts against my heart.

The picket-fence gate in front of the house—my nightmare ride—opens and closes in the wind. I move to stand in front of it, reaching for my aromatherapy necklace, suddenly reminded that I gave it to Parker. I keep grabbing for it, forgetting that it's no longer a part of me.

I move through the gate. The front door is already open. Still gripping the key, I head inside and go to flick on a light. But it isn't working. The windows have been covered over, too. The only light is from the open door.

I keep it propped open with a loose walkway brick, and then I move up the stairs, past the photos. The music grows louder with each step. My skin feels hot. The key is sweaty between my fingertips.

Just a step away from reaching the second floor, I hear a scuffling sound. It radiates down my spine. My mother screams. The front door slams behind me. More sounds follow: a bolt locking, glass breaking. Did someone throw a brick?

"Ivy?" Parker's voice. It's coming from outside.

"Your friend won't be able to get in," another voice whispers. *Garth?* Where is he?

My adrenaline racing, I climb another step looking all around.

Standing outside my parents' room, I wrap my hand around the knob, feeling my body tremble.

The knob turns. The door opens with a whine.

"Good evening, Princess," he says, his raspy voice speaking over the music.

It's my parents' killer. The birdlike eyes. The silver hair. He's got Parker in a headlock with a knife pressed against his neck. Wasn't Parker just outside? Is it possible that I heard wrong?

The killer smiles when he sees me, his head cocked to the side. "Welcome to the sequel."

I grip the key tighter. "I've been waiting for this moment," I tell him.

The comment takes him off guard. I can see it in the flutter of his eyelids, the swallowing in his throat.

Before he can rebound, I lunge forward, swiping at his face with the key. The motion causes him to release Parker.

I swipe at him again. This time I get his chest. He lets out a scream, but then I realize that I'm screaming too. I'm screaming as I cut him, as I stab him, as I plunge my key deep into his heart.

"Ivy!" Parker shouts, holding me back, taking the key, pinning my arms to the bed.

Someone else sits on my legs.

There's a hand on my forehead.

I wake up.

Parker isn't here.

It's Apple and Core, my foster parents. Rosie and Willow linger in the doorway, looking on.

I'm in my room. My covers are dark, dark blue. My walls are pale green and there are angled ceilings. A shag carpet covers the floor. And there's an armoire in place of a vanity. There are no soccer banners, nor is there a single reference to Katrina Rowe.

Apple gets up from my legs, sends Rosie and Willow back to bed, and then gently closes the door. Meanwhile, Core's got my knife—not a skeleton key—in his hands. My double-action switchblade; I've been keeping it beneath my pillow while I sleep.

Neither of them show alarm. Nights like this have been an all-too-regular occurrence—my subconscious wreaking havoc during my sleep, blurring the lines of reality, creating a mishmash of nightmarish visions from my nightmarish life. So far my parents have confiscated four knives and five keys, even though we were supposed to be playing by the "three strikes" rule.

Three strikes and they were going to check me in someplace, afraid that I might hurt myself, terrified that I might hurt one of the others. I can't really say I blame them.

"You know what this means," Core says, sadness in his voice.

Apple nods, her eyes filled with tears. But instead of talking about the consequences now, she crawls into my bed and holds on to me for dear life. For just a moment, I forget that she isn't my real mother.

I face the window as she snuggles me close. The breeze filters in through the window screen, and I can hear the sounds from outside: the tinkling of backyard wind chimes, the banging of shutters somewhere, and the rattling of overturned trash cans.

The musical score to *Haunt Me* still plays in my mind.

I vow to make it stop.

I vow to find Parker.

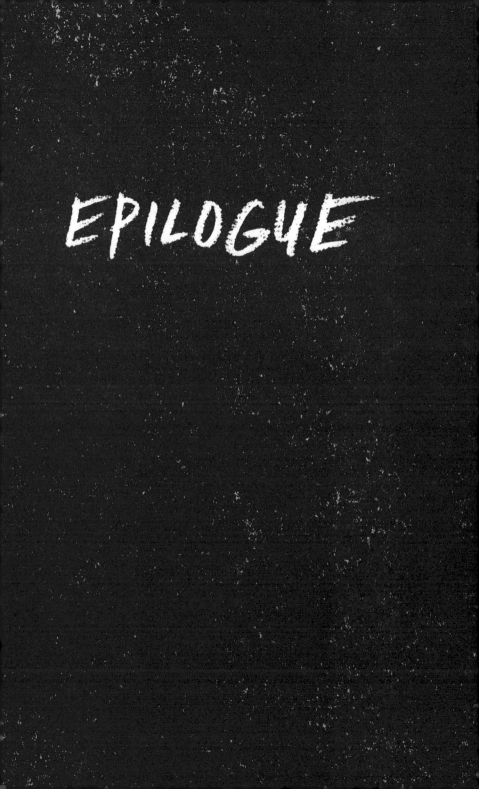

EPILOGUE

IVY

I REACH FOR THE LARGE MANILA ENVELOPE HIDDEN beneath my bed—a package that arrived last week. With no postmark and no return address, I assumed it was another anonymous gift from my parents' killer, like the pink soccer jersey from two years ago. But then I saw that my name and address were written in red crayon, just like the WELCOME TO THE DARK HOUSE sign, and I knew that wasn't the case.

I open the envelope and pull out the winning essays. A note attached to the first one reads *See you for the sequel, Princess.*

As has become my my bedtime ritual, I begin to reread:

In a thousand words or less, describe your worst nightmare.

By Frankie Rice

At five years old, I was too young to be at a wake, but I was, and I saw the body. Dressed in a navy blue suit and a slim red tie, Uncle Pete was no longer as I remembered him: the funny guy at the end of the dinner table telling jokes. Instead, he was lying in a box with no reason to laugh at all.

I climbed up on a stool to view the casket and focused on just his hands, unable to bring myself to look at his face. Gone were the oil stains from working on cars. His hands were cleaned, polished, and powdered. If it weren't for the watch around his wrist—the same braided leather one that my dad has—and his long, callused fingers, I'd have sworn those hands weren't his.

Dad said that Uncle Pete had died in his sleep from accidentally taking too many pills. I hated pills after that. I hated even more that his death came only a few months after my mother had walked out without so much as a good-bye.

Later, at the burial, I was surrounded by rows and rows of headstones, perched over hundreds of dead, buried bodies—proof positive that happily ever after doesn't exist.

I watched as they lowered Uncle Pete down into the ground, and a wave of panic struck me. What if my dad died in his sleep? Who would I have then? For as long as I could remember, Dad had been taking pills from the little brown bottle beside his bed.

I folded to the ground, a broken-glass sensation inside my chest. Soon, no one was paying attention to poor Uncle Pete, covered in dirt. They were focused on me, the five-year-old nephew, as I tried my hardest to breathe.

I passed out and was rushed to the hospital. Doctors insisted that I needed therapy, attention, and rest. Dad laughed at the first two suggestions. And that last one was impossible, because that's when my nightmares started.

That night, back at home, lying in bed, I kept a firm hold of my teddy bear—the blue one with no mouth (the threading tore) and only one eye—so that it wouldn't leave me too. I tossed and turned for hours.

The phone ringing finally pulled me out of bed. I was con-vinced that it was my mother calling to tell me where she was and that the phone extension was buried underground, right along with my uncle. If I wanted to speak to my mother again, I knew I had to dig up Uncle Pete's grave.

I walked past a long row of headstones. The ringing of the phone grew louder with each step. Tarantula-like trees bordered the cemetery on both sides. They looked like they could spring to life at any moment and take someone else from me.

I got down on my hands and knees as the phone continued to ring. "Don't hang up," I shouted to my mother. "I'm going as fast as I can." I dug my fingertips into the dirt, desperate to answer her call.

The dirt came up easily at first, but around three feet deep, my fingers started to burn. Still, I kept going, my wrists aching, my shoulders throbbing. My heart pounded as I got closer—just a few feet more. I climbed inside the hole, using my heels to dig in too.

Finally I got to the casket. With trembling hands, I lifted the cover.

Uncle Pete's eyes opened. "Hey, champ. I really dig it that you dug me out," he joked.

He'd been buried alive.

I couldn't stop shaking. Sitting at the foot of the casket, teetering on the frame, I stablized myself to keep from tumbling forward.

"Thanks so much for rescuing me," he continued. "I suppose now you'd like to answer the phone." The phone extension was in his grip—in his powdery white hand.

I reached out to take it. At the same moment, Uncle Pete

grabbed my arm and pulled me forward. I toppled on top of him.

The casket cover closed, locking me inside.

I woke up, out of breath, in my parents' bedroom closet. Two layers of skin had burned off my fingertips from digging into the carpeted floor.

The phone had stopped ringing by then, so I have no proof that it was my mother calling that night, but I have a strong suspicion that it was—that she wanted to say sorry about Uncle Pete.

I can't help but blame myself for missing that call—my one and only chance to get her back.

In a thousand words or less, describe your worst nightmare.

By Taylor Monroe

I should probably start off by saying that I hate camping— like, I really hate it. A deep-seated loathing that burrows to the depths of my soul. I'm not exaggerating, either. There's just so much to detest: sleeping in the woods, eating charcoal-blackened food, peeing in an outhouse, getting bitten by mosquitoes. I hate tents, dirt, greenhead flies, bug spray, lawn chairs, air mattresses, wild animals, and "Kumbaya" by the fire.

Of course, as luck would have it (please read sarcasm here), my parents insist that we go camping each year. This torture started at the age of eleven. I just turned eighteen (eighteen = a legal adult . . . and guess which legal adult will be exercising her right not to go camping this year). In case you haven't yet done the math, that's seven years of torture. Almost half of my life.

Don't get me wrong; I didn't always hate camping. That first year, I was really into it (or at least the idea of it). I had the dates marked on my calendar and I talked it up to friends, practically making myself out to be G. I. Jane, the star of the next hit reality TV show—one that has a wilderness theme. I was also packed and ready to go before anyone else in my family.

But then we got there and I discovered, much to my chagrin, that it wasn't at all like that episode of The Darkashians . . . when the family drove a luxury RV two hours outside of LA to set up camp and spend the night.

"Can you find us some long sticks?" Dad asked me on our first day there. He was standing by the fire, getting ready to make dinner, but he'd forgotten to pack skewers. "Six of them," he added.

With my mom and brother off swimming in the leech-infested lake, I had no other choice but to oblige. I abandoned my magazine and went up the trail, where we'd all hiked earlier in the day.

Trees and brush surrounded me on both sides of the path. With the sun sinking in the sky, peeking down through the limbs, I had to admit, the forest looked really striking.

I scanned the ground, searching for fallen sticks at least a couple feet in length. Maybe camping's not so bad, I thought, my mind flashing to the cute boy at the campsite next to ours. Maybe I'd ask him to toast marshmallows with *us later. I smiled at the idea, and then reached out to snag a curved branch, catching a glimpse of something brown and furry in the corner of my eye.*

I stopped to get a better look. Its eyes were watching me from beyond the tree, a stone's throw away.

A cub. So irresistibly cute, like something you'd see on the cover of National Geographic *or on that reality show* Super Cute. *The cub had a friend, who appeared to be cleaning himself off, licking his coat.*

I wondered if they were lost, but no sooner did that thought cross my mind than I spotted the mother. She emerged from some brush. And stared back at me.

My heart immediately sank. I didn't have time to react. There was a flash of fur, and the sound of a growl.

I was on the ground in seconds. The mother bear was on top of me, biting my arm, growling in my ear. Its razor-sharp teeth sank into my leg. It lifted me up and shook me from side to side, thrashing me around like a rag doll.

Surprisingly, I felt no pain. My body went into some sort of self-protective mode. I dropped to the ground, shielded my face, tucked into a fetal position.

But still the bear wouldn't let me go. It bit the corner of my mouth. Then my shoulder. And the back of my head. I could hear myself whimpering, could feel my body twitching. Its

claws ripped through my T-shirt, tearing up my skin.

My vision was blurry, but I was able to peek around me.

Blood was everywhere. I touched my shoulder, able to feel

bone. I was sure I was going to die.

I reached for a rock, but it was beyond my grasp. I needed

a few more inches.

The bear let out another roar before clawing at my side. I

could feel my skin rip free.

"Dad!" I tried to scream, but the word came out a wheeze.

Still, Dad was able to hear me. He shook me awake. I'd

been sleeping in my tent, having a bad dream. My mag-

azine was on the ground beside me, splayed open to an

article about bear attacks.

"Taylor, are you okay?" he asked.

I sat up, my heart pounding, my eye still blurred from my

being pressed against the pillow. I collapsed into my dad's

arms, feeling insurmountable relief.

He stroked my hair back and then started to pull away.

But I refused to let him go. "Can you just hold me for a little

while longer?"

"I'll hold you for as long as you want," he said, startled

that I'd gotten so freaked. (For the record, I don't

341

typically scare so easily; I mean, hello, I entered this contest, didn't I?)

Anyway, you'd think that after seeing how horrified his firstborn had become, he'd think twice about camping, right? No such luck.

In a thousand words or less, describe your worst nightmare.

By Garth Vader

I was seven years old when I got lost in the woods. It was during a camping trip with my dad and brothers. I woke up around two in the morning, needing to take a piss.

I grabbed a flashlight and walked down a dirt path, searching for the grove of trees, where my brothers and I had whizzed earlier in the day.

But I couldn't find it. Nor could I find my way back to the campsite.

"Craig?" I shouted, hoping to wake my brothers. "Paul?" Was this another one of my dad's tricks?

No one answered.

I hurried up and down the path, shining my flashlight over trees and brush, continuing to call out for help.

But no one came. And I was starting to panic.

Noises were coming from everywhere—sticks breaking, leaves shifting. Finally, after an hour of walking, I found a cabin. The windows were dark. Maybe the owners were sleeping. I shone my flashlight over the entrance. The

343

words *Welcome to the Dark House* were scribbled in red crayon.

I knocked and the door edged open. I went inside, hoping to find a phone.

A voice cut through the darkness: "Have you come to play?"

A creaking sound followed. I aimed my flashlight at a doll. The Nightmare Elf, rocking back and forth in a wooden rocking chair.

The door slammed behind me. The lock bolted shut. The elf's smile widened.

Desperate, I ran into a room with an open door, hoping to find a phone.

Little Sally Jacobs was there, sitting on the floor, playing a game of jacks. "Do you want to play?" She looked up at me with skeleton keys jammed into her eyes. Blood trickled down her cheeks. She went to remove one of the keys—a thick slopping sound.

I hurried to the window, but it was locked, and I couldn't get the bolt to unlatch.

I turned back around.

Sally was there. "Leaving so soon?" she asked, coming at me with the bloody key.

I ran to the closet, closing the door behind me, and keeping my hand on the knob.

The doorknob twisted beneath my grip; she was trying to get in. I clenched my teeth and struggled to hold the knob steady, my wrists aching, my forehead sweating.

Finally the knob stopped moving. I placed my ear against the door, unable to hear a peep.

My pulse racing, I searched for something to protect myself, noticing a secret door at the back of the closet. I opened it. A long, dark alleyway faced me, surrounded on both sides by tall brick buildings.

I began down the alley, able to hear a rattling sound. I peered over my shoulder just as a shopping cart came into view. A woman in a big blue dress was pushing it.

Lizzy Greer from Halls of Horror. *She turned to face me, pulling a bloodstained ax from the heap of soda cans in her cart. "Have you come to play?"*

My body began to shake. I dropped my flashlight and tried to run past her, rounding a corner, spotting the rear door of Hotel 9. I tore through it and mounted a flight of stairs.

Someone was following me. I could hear the sound of footsteps, the creaking of a rocking chair, the bouncing of Little Sally Jacobs's ball, and the rattle of Lizzy's cart.

"Come play with us," their voices said.

I ran into one of the hotel rooms, locked the door, and hid beneath the bed. That's when I completely lost it—right there in the middle of my dream, I pissed on the sofa.

I used to get a variation of that nightmare a few times a week. Sometimes Pudgy the Clown would show up with his chain saw; other times, it'd be Sidney Scarcella wearing his butler's apron, or Sebastian Slayer in that scene where he plays the piano in the middle of the forest with severed body parts strewn about.

It was on my seventh birthday that I first saw the original Nightmare Elf *movie. My dad had dared me, saying that it was the only way I could prove I wasn't still a baby. Pretty screwed up, I know. But that's my dad for you.*

He and my brothers had watched a bunch more of your films that night. And me, being too chickenshit to go up to my room after seeing Nightmare Elf, *I brought a sleeping bag into the TV room so I wouldn't have to be alone.*

Keeping my head beneath the covers, I tried not to peek at the screen, even when my dad bribed me with money, candy, and days off from school.

But I also didn't want to be a baby. I wanted to make him proud—to this day, I've yet to succeed.

346

For a while, I was sleeping under my bed, paranoid that the Nightmare Elf would take my dreams and make them come true.

The more fearful I became, the worse things got at home. My dad would call me pansy, pretty girl, baby, and sweet pea. He'd give me a baby cup at dinner and point me toward the girls' room when we were out in public. Finally, when I couldn't take his teasing anymore, I started watching more horror flicks—as many as I could get my hands on.

In the end, I grew to love horror just as much as my dad, probably even more because it became a part of my identity. Incidentally, in case you hadn't already noticed, I was named after my dad's all-time favorite villain—with one obvious adjustment, that is. He would've gone full out and named me Darth, but luckily my mom won that coin toss.

In a thousand words or less, describe your worst nightmare.

By Natalie Sorrento

I have nightmares about my reflection—about seeing myself, that is. They started two years ago, after my sister Margie caught me with my pants down—literally—after I'd just come out of the shower.

Standing naked, I was about to look at myself in the full-length mirror on the back of the door, but the steam from the shower had fogged up the glass. So I gazed downward at my thighs—at my very first tattoos. They were newly done and deliciously red and sting-y.

A moment later, the bathroom door whipped open. "Gross," Margie said, shielding her eyes from the sight of me. But still she was able to find my newly inked tattoos through the spaces between her chocolate-stained fingers. "What are those?" A megawatt grin formed on her face, like she'd just struck the blackmailing lottery. If only she'd wanted to blackmail me.

Instead, she went straight to my parents and pulled them into the bathroom. I'd managed to grab a towel, but my dad ripped it out of my hands. And they all stared, open mouthed.

At me. Naked. At my paunchy gut, my cottage-cheese legs, and the bloody tattoos on my thighs: Lizzy Greer's ax on one thigh, and the infamous door-with-a-peephole from Hotel 9 on the other.

I tried to cover up as best I could, cupping my hands over my boobs and crotch, while holding back hot, bubbling tears. But it wasn't nearly enough. And their expressions confirmed what I already knew. I was undeniably hideous. Deplorable. Hopeless. Regrettable.

Mom: "How did this happen?"

Dad: "If only . . ."

Ever since that day, I've avoided mirrors. I keep a desk blotter over the vanity in my bedroom. I close my eyes as I wash my hands in bathrooms. I never stand or walk too close to windows or glass doors, for fear of seeing a reflection. And I'm careful not to go into places that are known to have mirrors, e.g., hair salons, dressing rooms, department stores, and gyms.

I also avoid having my picture taken, including for class photos. I've ditched school on picture day for the past several years. Nobody's ever questioned it—nobody gives a shit that I'm not standing with my classmates, a fake smile across my zit-covered face.

Lastly, I keep myself covered—tattoos, wigs, sunglasses,

layers of clothing—so that no one has to see me. And so that I, in turn, never have to see the reflection of myself in anyone else's eyes.

But at night, I can't escape my reflection. I have night- mares about being trapped inside a maze of mirrors, unable to find my way out. With each corner I turn, my image gets uglier and more distorted—one moment short and bulging, the next stretched out and warped.

The images accentuate what's wrong with me: face too long, eyes too big, hair too frizzy, crooked nose, fishlike lips, hips too wide, waist too thick, chunky knees, pasty skin. In my dream, I try to run away from the images, but they're everywhere, chasing me, laughing at me. I move to the side—into yet another mirror—as if that one will make a difference. And it does. It's the worst image yet. It's the real me, in a real mirror—far worse than any distortion.

In a thousand words or less, describe your worst nightmare.

By Parker Bradley

Its teeth sank into my leg—a tearing, mind-blowing pain. Despite not being in the ocean, I thought it was a shark. But then its body crested the surface of the water, and I saw what it really was.

An eel—at least six feet long and five inches wide. Its mouth arched open—dozens of razor-sharp teeth snapped at my ribs. I tried to get away, but it was too big, too fast. The next thing I knew, I was underwater.

In my mind, I screamed for help. In reality, I couldn't breathe, couldn't scream. Somehow I managed to paddle upward, and the eel lost its grip on my side. I started to move away. But then it bit my thigh—deep into the flesh— pulling me back under.

My mouth filled up with water. Everything around me turned red. Out of the corner of my eye, I saw something move over the surface of the water. An oil spill? A liquid of some sort? It was spreading like lava.

I broke through the surface again, able to see just what it was—not a liquid at all.

A steel cover extended over the entire width of the pond. The cover was moving closer, forming a lid over the water's surface. If I didn't get out, I'd be trapped underneath it.

More eels came, at least twenty of them, swarming me, tearing into my back, my chest, my legs, my feet. They pulled me under once more.

I looked up. The cover was above my head. I tried to push on it, but it wouldn't budge.

I paddled fast, chasing the edge of the cover, scrambling to get in front of it. But it was too late. The pond was completely sealed now.

I screamed beneath the surface of the water, this time able to hear my voice—a sharp, piercing wail that woke me up.

I was in the hospital, lying in bed, having a nightmare about something that had happened the day before. My legs were covered in bite marks.

A nurse was sitting beside me. "You had another one, huh?" she asked.

I nodded. It was my third nightmare that night.

"Those nasty dreams will fade with time."

If only that were true.

I had nearly drowned. It happened at summer camp,

when I was ten years old, after most of the other campers had already been picked up for the day. I was left waiting for my ride.

It was hot out, but since I didn't know how to swim, the counselors had forbidden me from going into the water. Even earlier in the day, when all of my fellow campers had free swim, I'd been given a squirt gun and a bucket of water, and told to keep cool.

But being the end of the day, the counselors had gone back to the office to clean up. So, I jumped right into the pond, and started paddling around. But no sooner did I get out chest-deep than I felt that first rip.

It took my brain a beat to catch up to the sensation. And when it did, I heard a yell, realizing it was mine. My voice. My panic. Like an out-of-body experience.

Water was splashing all around me—I was doing that, too—trying to get out, to get away.

But something still had my calf.

And clouds of red colored the water.

Eventually people came. There were sirens and flashing lights. Arms were reaching, pulling, tugging, twisting. Voices were shouting directives. All the fight I had was gone.

Months later, I did a report on eels in school. I learned that it's only in extreme situations that eels attack humans. Like, if the eels are feeding and someone gets caught up in the midst, or if the eels are caged and starved. Though some-what reassuring, I haven't entered the water since. And I know I never will.

In a thousand words or less, describe your worst nightmare.

By Shayla Belmont

I was the one who found Dara's body. She'd hung herself in the closet, in her dorm room, at our boarding school—the same boarding school I'd convinced her to transfer to with the promise of cute boys, weekends in the city, and pizza-and-Chinese-food-flavored cram sessions.

Her feet dangled above the floor. She was wearing her heart-patterned socks—the same ones that we both owned from a trip to the mall months before when we'd bought matching pairs. Standing there, I had to wonder if she'd worn those socks on purpose, if she'd banked on me being the one to find her. Was that her way of forcing me to remember the way things used to be?

Her face was bluish gray. Her eyes were open, focused upward. The telephone wire wrapped around her neck had cut into her throat. I reached out to touch her hand, notic-ing that the blood from her arms had drained down to her fingertips.

That's when I knew for sure. It's when I felt my legs give way beneath me. My best friend Dara was dead.

I was nine years old when we met. It was at yoga camp in the Berkshires and we got partnered up by Saffron, the yoga master who insisted that Dara and I had the same karmic energy and were destined to be best friends. Little did I know that Saffron would be right. Little did I know that seven years of best friendship later, Dara would end up taking her own life. Where was her karmic energy then?

I've heard stories that your life flashes before you in those fleeting seconds before death. I wasn't physically dying in that moment, but emotionally I guess I was. Images of Dara and me raced across my mind: at thirteen years old, dyeing our hair green for St. Patrick's Day; dance parties in her basement; mini-makeovers in my bedroom; hot-fudge-sundae-with-whipped-cream pacts that we'd always be there for each other, no matter what.

I looked up at her face again. Her lips were chalky white, parted open, exposing the familiar gap in her front teeth, where she'd once stuck a Cheez-It to be funny. Her long orange hair was in a sideways braid.

The nightmares that I have about Dara are always the same—always me, searching for her. There's always a long, dark hallway, like in the resident dorm at night. I go to her room and open the closet.

And there's her body. Those heart-patterned socks.

Though, in the dream, her eyes are closed. And instead of fond memories flashing before my eyes, I'm haunted by those moments when I could've been a better friend. Like the time I left her teary eyed on my doorstep because I had dinner plans with Miranda and Gigi.

And the time I told her I was too sick to spend the weekend watching movies and giving each other mani-pedicures, as planned, because I'd been invited up to Bunny's ski house.

And then, just when things can't get any more hideous—and I'm unable to force myself to wake up—her eyelids snap open and she stares back at me.

"I thought we were supposed to be friends," she whispers, tears dripping down her face.

I open my mouth to tell her that we are friends, that she'll always be my best friend, but the words won't come out; they remain stuck inside my head.

Her arm raises up then, and she points in my direction with her dark blue finger. Her lips are pursed; her eyes are wide and teary. She's angry and sad at the same time. "You weren't there for me," she says. "You broke your promise. And now you'll pay."

ACKNOWLEDGMENTS

A VERY SPECIAL THANK-YOU TO CHRISTIAN TRIMMER, my brilliantly talented editor of five years. I'm so grateful to have worked with you. Thank you for acquiring this project and beginning its editorial journey with me.

Huge thanks to Tracey Keevan, who continued with me on that journey, working round the clock, cheering me on, and pushing me harder—my very own literary personal trainer. This book is so much stronger because of you.

Thanks to Kathryn Green, agent extraordinaire. I'm so grateful to have you in my corner. A million thanks for all you do.

Special thanks to music guru Frankie Price for answering all of my guitar- and music-related questions. Any related errors found within this novel are mine and mine alone.

Thank you to all of the friends and family members who offer to read drafts of my work and who give me time to write as well as cups of fresh coffee (black, no sugar).

And lastly, a very special thank-you to my readers, who continue to support my work and cheer me on. You guys are the absolute best.